Down in the ditch, Sandal looked dazed; Marty propped his arm behind her shoulders. "Sonsabitches got away," she mumbled, spitting dirt and rubbing her elbow. "I just about had 'em, only I hit the new cut at the tree line and nearly broke my neck."

"How many were there?" I wished for a flashlight.

"I saw two."

Gravel showered down on us as Gladdie rumbled into the ditch. "You okay, hon? They hurt you?" She reached for Sandal, and brushed at her face.

"Hell, I hurt myself trying to catch up to them. They must be track stars."

"You hit anyone?" Marty asked, eyeing the shotgun.

"No, I just wanted to scare them."

"How many did you see?" I asked her.

"Two, but not close up."

Sandal leaned her head on Gladdie's breast. "Did you see what they did to my stone? Sonsabitches bashed in one of her breasts."

Gladdie stroked her hair. Starlight flashed off her gun barrel. "She'll be all right."

"Hell yes," Marty confirmed. "She's an Amazon."

Other Naiad books by Vicki P. McConnell

Mrs. Porter's Letter

The Burnton Widows

Double Daughter

Berrigan (Forthcoming)

Author's Briefs

In second grade, I starred in the play "Gay Bunny." In high school, I was voted Best Thespian. In college, Best Actress. We all know it can sometimes be critical to play a part.

I used to do sports and ride a motorcycle. I once played the cello, which I named Floyd. On guitar, I learned three chords. I wanted to play sax like Boots, but could only manage a bad version of "America the Beautiful." You guessed it — music wasn't my deal.

One of my first published works was a poem about the Beatles in *Teen Life*.

I have a Bachelor's degree in Theatre/English, and two international ADDC writing awards. I'm a nearly-40 Libran who *can* make a decision.

I've been known to nap under my fish tank so I could watch them all swimming upside down. I like a unique perspective.

My father once said gay people leave a trail. Writing is finding a trail through the mystery of life. Damned proud work.

Vicki P. McConnell

ILLUSTRATOR Janet Fons (B.F.A., Michigan State University in Print Making/Graphic Design) has nearly 15 years' experience in graphics and illustration. Currently an art director for a Denver design firm, her work appears in the other Nyla Wade mysteries. A regional/national award winner in design and advertising, Janet is now marketing her fine art commercially.

DOUBLE DAUGHTER

VICKI P. MCCONNELL

Illustrated by Janet Fons

THE NAIAD PRESS INC.

Printed in the United States of America
First Edition

Edited by Katherine V. Forrest
Cover design and interior illustrations by Janet Fons
Typesetting by Sandi Stancil

Library of Congress Cataloging-in-Publication Data

McConnell, Vicki P.
    Double daughter / by Vicki P. McConnell.
        p. cm.
    ISBN 0-941483-26-6
    I. Title.
PS3563.C344D68 1988
813'.54--dc 19   88-23605
                                                          CIP

DEDICATION

To the storm goddess Dike, warrior/avenger, who carried the long spear.

To my family:
DOROTHY ROSE — unafraid to keep learning, her laughter is a magical chime of love.
MAURILYN DENISE — my spirit sister, brave enough to travel the portals with me, sweet enough to cry for my pains.
DEIRDRE REILLY — for generosity, fearless driving, and the amethyst tree.
SANDRA LEE JONES — our one and only Indian Princess.
NANCY WHITE — who brought forth the turquoise notebook.
And LOTUS — poet, her own kind of warrior.

MERCI TO:
Polly Hinds and Lynda German (for the critical loan of their computer to birth this book); Cecil Dawkins (early editing); Katherine Forrest (polish and praise).

My patient and caring readers: Mom, Dierdre, Connie, Mel White, June Summers, Josie Prach, Ronnie Storey, Adrienne St. Clair, Neil Woodward, Penny Salazar, and Polly and Lynda.

Spiritual support from Janet Fons (for imaging the images); Liv Edwards (heartbeat books, and planets);

Roberta Parry (the West Bank book); Gina Miller (romantic review); Anne Hinson (work on patterns, and holding); Judy Cooper (the White Knightess); Josie (for idealism and "aching flowers"); Anne L. Rosenblum (for bodyguarding); from the days of the *Oklahoma Gaily,* Susan Bishop; Neil and Dan at Category Six; Lynn Kelsey; Sharon Bean and Bea Gotschall (sisters of wheat); Karen Brungardt; Katie O (you give good float); Judy Bucher; Sharon Silvas; Barbara Smith (for the Franklin house sanctuary); Gail McLelland; Pat Delbridge (who asked to be my champion); the real Audrey Louise, wherever she is; Maggie Harrison's line from "In a German Cemetary"; and Sally Morgan and my friends in the channeling circles, for lessons in love.

For research help — Linda Felicio (cop talk); Connie (fire talk); Gail and Nancy (medical talk); Carla Covelli (postperson talk); Jerry Hunter (computer talk); Lt. Tom Haney of the Denver Police Homicide Dept.; Tom Hagney at the Denver Crime Lab; Eric Parker (*Times-Call*/Boulder); S.R.; Marilyn Robinson, Carol Krek, and Tom Graff (*The Denver Post*); Fran and Ralph Welte for the special tour of their brick company and museum in Pueblo; Shirley Hunter (also for brick adventures); Tracy Anderson at the GLCC; Carol A. Polevoy and Katie O'Brien (legal assistance); and Neil Woodward (specialty info).

To some special Aurora wimmin: K.C. — Aurora to Key West, for peeling oranges and other sweets; and two friends of old who actually live in that lesser suburb: Ann Klotz and Charlotte Mervin.

In memory of Wayne John; Shep Holderby; Sarah J. Myers; John L. and Denny W.; our own Challengers, S. Christa McAuliffe and Judy Resnick; tiny Tina and Natalie W., who went down with the ships; and Dulcie September, who did not die in silence.

To Yoko (for taking heat), to Whoopie (for giving heat), to Martina (for rushing the net).

I hope you will be a warrior and fierce for change, so all can live.
> —Meridel LeSeur, "Annunciation"

To all wimmin warriors everywhere — the fight is forever, but we never journey alone.

CONTENTS

PRELUDE

When Lucy peeled off her shirt and flexed her shoulders, I wanted to polish that favorite skin with my fingers. Feel the special lift of strength in her arms. Make wild butterflies down between her breasts.

Just a week ago she'd bent her shoulders into shoveling through the ashes of the Burnton, Oregon Women's Center. We found the charred cashbox full of soot and nickels. We dug up the small cornerstone. Ten years of memories echoed out of those cinders — Rita Mae Brown had sent a rubyfruit basket for the opening, Adrienne Rich had read all twenty-one love poems from

1

the softness of the donated sofa. Endless bake sales and walkathons had kept the doors open, and lives had been saved because of that space. A shared passion had ignited there and kindled for an era, then burned out with a cruel finality.

I'd covered Center events for the *Beckoner* newspaper because I believed the continuing effort there was important news. And because my own life had changed in loving women and loving Lucy. Yet now when I felt a fire of rage about the burning, she didn't even cry. She kept her reactions to herself — whether silent grief or anger, I didn't know. I only knew that for the first time in two years, we couldn't talk.

So I reached for her now with a desperate heart, and I made love scared. A little too hard and fast, like my bones were loose and our bed was an edge into darkness where I might fall forever. I found her skin through a fog, broke cries into her for comfort and connection. Moved over her like a quick night flare, hot and bright but hopeless against the stars.

1
ENTER NYLA WADE

I left for Denver in the morning. We stood apart in the lobby of the Coos Bay airport. As I thought about sleeping without her, she tried to tease me.

"In two weeks I'll come to Colorado, and we'll climb Dyke's Peak."

"That's Pike's Peak, Lucy."

"Only till I get there."

I wanted to believe she would get there in time. My flight was called, and we looked at each other. What

3

greater risk in this parting, beyond the stares of other travelers? She opened her arms and turned her face for the proof of a kiss. I left the shadow of my lips at the corner of her mouth.

When the plane dropped toward the grey top hats of the Rockies, I was dreaming a poem from my college days.

> Lesbian — the word is my warpaint.
> A swipe on each cheek for valor.
> Lesbian — the word I wear on my face
> And in my willful heart.
> Lesbian — the lion who sleeps with lambs.

Seat me with the lambs, I sighed. The poem was the first I'd ever heard that proudly used the word and named the fight. Written by one of my classmates, a modern Amazon I'd called her then. Did she still herald the cause? Burnton had its own Amazon — my friend Judge Lynda Carruthers. She too had helped shovel through the Center's ashes. And though steeped in the daily trials of man's inhumanity to man, woman, and child, she held onto her ideals, still called feminists "the modern warriors," still rallied us to "the privilege of duty, carrying the long spear."

But I didn't feel like a warrior. I felt full of fear and questions. I had a hole inside me big as that burned black square of cinders. Once I'd been filled by my sure knowledge that my woman lover and I could meet any problem and solve it together, that working for the needs of women could make a difference. Now a case of faulty wiring felt like a message from the gods. Burned up or burned out, could we ever fight fire with spears?

4

* * * * *

Audrey Louise did a Tarzan yell when she spotted me on the concourse. We ran to each other and hugged and cried, made a scene all the way to Baggage Claim. Best friends have such rights.

"You look great," I told her as we stepped onto the escalator, though her mascara had made false bruises under her eyes. "Svelte and sassy."

She shook me by my sleeve. "I'm still mad that you moved. How's Lucy?"

I didn't have to answer because we stepped into the dungeon of suitcases, and I heard her oldest son, Sam.

"I see her, I see her first!"

"Did not, I see her too!" middle-son Mark protested. They ran toward us, jostling everyone.

"Enter the tribe," Audrey Louise joked.

I gave her husband Joel a hug, smelled cherryroot pipe smoke in his shirt. "Wait a second, someone's missing. Where's that Tony boy?"

Audrey Louise's youngest son peeked around from behind his father, blushing and silent, just handing me a bouquet of lavender carnations.

We headed for the Landry home in Aurora. I'd always teased Audrey Louise about living in the lesser suburbs. "Halfway to Kansas clear out there," I'd grump. "Kansas, home state of Amelia Earhart," she'd counter.

I asked, "Have you made all your plans for your birthday bash? Turning forty deserves a chorus line of dancing boys in jockey straps, and a naked man jumping out of a cake."

"I vote for the jockey straps," Joel said with a laugh. "With sequins. Or maybe see-through."

5

"No, Mom, have the naked man!" Sam hooted from the back seat.

"Naked jockey strap!" Mark echoed.

Audrey Louise just shook her head at them and squeezed my arm. "We're having a ton of melon balls and some people we knew in college."

"Oh lord," I groaned. "Not anyone who knows my checkered past, I hope."

"You might be surprised."

Leave it to suburbia to take the edge off greater concerns. The beige brick house fronted with grass bright as new paint cheered me. Joel and Audrey Louise had built a guest apartment over their garage. They gave me full run of it.

"Glad you're bunking in with us." Joel grinned and reached for Audrey Louise. "The wife couldn't sleep a wink last night waiting to see you. I thank you for that."

She poked his arm. "Come on, Joel, help me make dinner before everyone starves." They started for the house, then she turned back, gave me a hug, and said, "Damn, I'm glad you're here."

The garage apartment offered every amenity, including a nifty cooking nook with mini-fridge and microwave. I opened sliding glass doors next to the bed and went out onto a redwood deck. To my surprise, there below was the aqua oval of a new swimming pool.

Looking into the water, I realized suddenly the absence of the surf — a sound in Oregon that had become part of my own pulse. And then I felt the mountains around me. They did not hide or shun even Aurora, and now they were sun-girdled and ready to toss the moon up from their black shoulders. I smelled the cool-dust tinge of

Spring rain coming. This would be my first night sleeping alone in two years — no ocean's rhythm, no Lucy spooning my back. Or loving me in her wonder-child way, with fearless hands seeking magic. Until this blackout of our souls.

2
HOTSPUR

When I awakened, a fine web of sunlight shimmered around my hand. I missed rolling toward Lucy and saying I love you. The sound of splashing water urged me, naked, out onto the deck.

Audrey Louise was walking a slow circle around the pool, running a net to catch up leaves and twigs from last night's rain. It was almost like a meditation, her fluid movement with the net stroking the water. The heat pump for the pool shushed in friendly burps, the grass sparkled. Perhaps Audrey Louise was my meditation in this lifetime.

She shaded her eyes and stared up at me. "Nice outfit."

I laughed, remembering days when we were young and modest.

"Grab a robe and let's have coffee. It's a big day for making melon balls."

The house sounded too quiet, but I followed the smell of coffee. "Where is everyone?"

"Off to their Saturday wars." She was already peeling the rind off cantaloupes.

I gave her a hug. "Then we're alone and you can tell me the truth. Are you having an age crisis?"

She laughed, and the sound rang into me like a long lost chime. "Get serious. I get better every year. Ask Joel — he can barely catch his breath." She nudged a honeydew toward me.

For a moment, a vision of the Center's ashes flooded my mind. "Maybe *I'm* the one having the age crisis. I feel like a zealot who bloomed too late."

"You were always a zealot, Nyla. That picture over by the window proves it."

She'd framed an old photo from the Denver Community College *Clarion*. "Nyla Wade does beehive," I said. "How dreadful."

"Forget the hairdo, read the caption."

"Senior Nyla Wade receives the state first place award for College Newswriting from Dr. Martin J. Evans."

"For your exposé on discrimination against women officers in the ROTC program. You gave those soldier girls a voice."

My own voice felt like a whisper. "Marty Evans, Mr. Journalism himself."

"You always said he was strong and sensitive."

"How profound. If I said that now, I'd probably think he was gay."

Audrey Louise made a melon-ball flowerette and popped it into my mouth. "As a matter of fact, he is."

We'd had our suspicions when Marty Evans was guru to a group of us called the Passionate Few. D.C.C. students and teachers during the intensely liberal early 70s — we believed that in all of Denver, or maybe the world, but certainly including the suburbs, we formed the hottest spot. A magnet for the Muse to drop her cosmic tether of enlightenment upon true *artistes*.

I wrote fervent political essays; Audrey Louise painted cloth art that looked like spaghetti and sex. We met every week at the home of Lois Stanley-Lewelyn, or Lois-Stan as we called her. To the manor born, she was, though her mansion sat in Aurora. We forgave her suburbia because she was the consummate hostess. Confined to a wheelchair by debilitative arthritis, she loved to laugh and to tell us her dreams about flying. And she championed our dear Dr. Evans as the icon of intellect and creative genius. She was his sponsor, he our mentor, and we hung on their every word.

"Marty did like to quote Oscar Wilde," I remembered.

"And Ferlinghetti. Verses about 'the dark passion of the ancients.' " Audrey Louise grinned and raised her eyebrows.

"So how did you scope out Marty's darker passions?"

"We got reacquainted at some alumni thing last year. He needed a grading assistant, so I volunteered. Maturity counts, you know. Now that we're peers, we can talk about our lives. He's pretty open. Especially after the book."

"What book?"

"Erotic poetry dedicated to him by his lover." She surveyed her bowl of bright fruit flowerettes, then gave me an ornery grin. *White Boys in Love.*

The hubbub of party preparations ended our reminiscence. Especially when the tribe returned to help. Sam banged around the furniture with the vacuum. Mark threw a fit about the pink and grey streamers, calling them "fairy colors, foo-foo like poodles with bows. People will think we're fairies!" Audrey Louise regaled him about the Good Fairy and the Tooth Fairy, but he stamped his foot. She swatted him once, and he gave up his indignation. Joel stocked the bar and smeared cream cheese into celery sticks.

While I dusted and retaped the crooked streamers, I remembered more about the Passionate Few. We had two English profs, one from Georgia and the other from Alabama, who prowled garage sales together looking for antique books. Lizbeth was complex and closed, a chain-smoker. Adelle wore a poncho and shared poems in her Southern accent about the odd iron spikes in German cemeteries and the "hard lace names" on women's graves. Red-haired and raw-boned Myrna created crisp, fast lyrics that we called her camera shutter poems. A girl from Nebraska made us laugh with stories about her Grandma's mud pies. She was always working four jobs at once. One summer as a lifeguard, she got completely sunburned except for a spot on her nose covered with blue lotion. We called her C.B. from then on, for Crispy Brown.

I touched one of the streamers. It felt like a lifeline back to that passionate time and our passionate few. Especially the modern Amazon, who had ignited our rebellion and touched our deeper emotions with her

11

images of Lesbian warpaint and gentle lions. No claim of love's dark side in her proud words. "Our hotspur," Lois Stan had nicknamed her. And for a moment I was back in that Aurora manor listening to Pat Stevens.

"Lesbians, the Mother Race, we will be slaves no more. We will bare our proud breasts to the moon, open our power to each other, flow like gold water, like a Womon River."

I needed to drink from that river now.

Dr. Martin Evans still held a dazzling sheen of energy in his green eyes. He brought Audrey Louise an armful of birthday gladiolus. Gave me a bearhug. I felt his full beard on my cheek. A touch of grey ran through his hair back to a small ponytail at his collar. I laughed and gave it a tug. "Professor Punker!"

"Surely I've stepped back in time. To the days of the Passionate Few."

"Sans a few of the few," I said. "Have you kept track of us?"

"Most of you. Except that girl obsessed with child suicide themes. And Camilla, do you remember her?"

"Didn't she write veiled poetry about her affair with a married man?"

"Don't count on Nyla to remember," Audrey Louise teased. "She was writing her own veiled poetry about Lizbeth and Adelle."

She left to answer the doorbell; Marty and I went into the living room. "What's become of the two Southern belles?" I asked him.

"Lizbeth teaches somewhere in Missouri. Adelle got married and settled into a rock farmhouse in Iowa."

"I'm surprised. I figured they'd end up somewhere together. What about Lois Stan? And C.B.?"

"Lois Stan died last year. But she kept on flying right up to the end. Had a license tag put on her wheelchair — 'Chariot of Fire.' As for our Nebraska farm girl . . ." He looked toward the hallway. "She can tell you herself."

Two women swirled into the living room in a march of color. One, reed tall and bean brown, wore a purple poncho slashed with yellow stripes. The other, round and smooth and porcelain white, had on a lime green muu-muu.

"Crispy Brown!" I hooted, and embraced the tall woman.

"You're a sight for sore eyes, Nyla Wade." She draped me in her purple, and introduced her companion. "This is Gladdie Aimwell, my partner." Then she hugged my waist and swished her poncho. "Remember ponchos? Adelle always wore one."

"So you had a crush on her too?" Audrey Louise teased.

"Didn't we all?"

"Are you still chasing four careers at once?" I asked.

"No, I've settled on being a sculptor. And I go by my given name now that I'm famous. Ms. Sandal Morgan, if you please." She twirled the poncho in a mock bow.

"More like infamous," Marty told me. "Central Bank commissioned her to do a piece on prosperity. She gave them a high-tech metal Medusa."

"Which they loved in spite of themselves," Sandal countered, sitting on the loveseat with Gladdie next to her. "Gladdie predicted they would." She squeezed her lover's hand and said, "We met at a psychic channeling."

Marty winked at me. Joel played happy butler with a tray of wieners in sauce. "Drinks all around. What can I

13

get you?" Audrey Louise proffered the first bowl of melon delights. "Happy tropical birthday," Gladdie laughed over the flowerettes.

"What about you, Nyla? Going to win a Pulitzer soon?" Sandal asked.

"I give it good odds," Marty answered before I could. "She was nominated for a Hearst award last year. Castles and coverups in Oregon."

"Sounds all gothic and criminal," Gladdie said. I liked her smiling eyes.

"*My* partner, Lucy Randolph, helped me solve that mystery. As well as a few others."

Sandal grinned at Marty. Joel returned with the drinks. We toasted old friends and mutual discoveries. Our jovial reunion continued over salmon dip and the celery sticks. Sandal asked if Audrey Louise still painted.

"About once a year. Pastoral scenes mostly. My brush is at peace." She chuckled.

Sandal talked about her new sculpture. "A stone Amazon. Twelve feet tall, size ten feet. Hips that could move a mountain, breasts to suckle the Universe."

Gladdie started telling us about transporting the stone when the doorbell rang. I wondered if Sandal would let the Amazon wear warpaint. Or perhaps she too birthed more peaceful art nowadays. "Sorry I'm late," I heard a woman say. "Something came up that I had to take care of." I looked toward the doorway and our newest guest. Recognized at once that toss of hair, like a fierce pony chasing a frothy wave. Or a womon river.

"Pat." Marty beamed.

"Hotspur," I breathed.

* * * * *

14

From the moment Pat Stevens joined us, I moved in a strange duality of time. She had changed so much. She floated in a double image before me — the warrior persona from my past, and the restrained woman in Audrey Louise's living room. No spark flared in her. No laughter lit her eyes. She seemed distracted, and even Marty did not put her at ease. He told us she was grooming new poets at D.C.C.

"Your turn to coach the young zealots." Sandal grinned.

"Most of them are materialists," Pat snapped. I caught a surprised glance from Audrey Louise.

Sandal tried again. "I understand you and Lois Stan stayed close. How did she stand that pain for so many years?"

"Mostly in silence. And diversion. We read to each other a lot. She had a weakness for poets. Last year she funded publishing a local woman named Gingerlox. Lois Stan said the name sounded like a gourmet cookie."

"One May Day she made each of us a paper rose," Sandal recalled. "And inside she'd copied one of your poems."

The memory touched Pat. And all of us who were remembering our friend.

Audrey Louise sought a lift in the mood. "I think it's fitting that in my fortieth year the Oxford English Dictionary has officially recognized the word *wimmin*."

"And the feds have sanctioned Ms.," Marty added.

"A bonus year," Sandal toasted.

"Change the language, change the world. We believed that." Pat looked into her scotch.

"Change the *men*, change the world, that's what you believed," Marty teased her. "You signed me up for a sensitivity group. I barely escaped alive!"

15

Finally Pat laughed.

"I keep thinking I'll find your name on the bestseller lists, Pat. Have you published?" Sandal asked.

"Only in Lois Stan's paper roses."

"That's not true," Marty said. "Your purple prose burned up the pages of the alternative press for years." He chuckled. "Then you went into your respectable phase. Under the dominion of Lou Diablo."

Another name from our shared past at D.C.C. "Louisa Diablo," I sighed. "The fantasy womon of my entire junior class. The Aphrodite of Archaeology. Everyone wanted to go down the Nile with her. Is she still at the college?"

Neither Marty nor Pat answered. They seemed to avoid each other's eyes. Audrey Louise finally said, "She went to Boston College last year."

"For tenure? More money, new love?" I persisted. "She was here a long time. I'd have thought this was her home by now."

"It was." Pat's tone had a hard edge. "I shared it for ten years. Then she wanted new territory."

Obviously I'd broached a touchy subject. Before I could change it, Marty made things worse.

"Muchas Macha, I called her. She was the faculty champion. Always willing to buck the regents for more money."

"White Bread, she called you," Pat said, her eyes on him in challenge.

"Sounds like friendly adversaries," Gladdie observed.

"Once we were friends." He looked at Pat as if to make peace. She didn't soften. Suddenly we were the Awkward Few.

"Speaking of peace, Marty, have you had any since *White Boys in Love*?" Count on Audrey Louise to restore the mood.

He laughed and I asked, "How did they take that at D.C.C. — did all the deans revolt?"

"Mostly they made jokes at my expense. And I foxed them all by laughing. A man wrote that he loved me — I was ecstatic, my peers were jealous. So the joke was really on them."

"No reprisals, no hate mail?"

I saw Pat tense up at Sandal's question.

"Nothing of the kind," Marty answered. "And these days my niche at the college is mighty comfy. Low class load, lots of honors students, time to theorize with the few non-materialists."

Pat didn't take his bait. Instead she headed to the kitchen for another drink. I followed her.

"Listen Pat, I'm sorry if I was out of line about Lou Diablo. I didn't know about you two. I would never have —"

"It's okay. I shouldn't be so sensitive. After all, it's been a year."

Since when did one year heal ten? I wondered. Pat said, "Marty and his white boys in love. Some people hate that love."

"What do you mean? Are there homophobes loose at D.C.C.?"

"I just mean not everyone is comfortable about gay teachers."

I wanted to ask who she meant specifically, but her tone didn't invite such inquiry. She surprised me then, saying, "I remember your poem for Janis Joplin." In that moment, I couldn't remember it myself.

* * * * *

The Passionate Few finished the evening by conceding that we would not toast Audrey Louise forty times and still be standing. Yet we affirmed that age had made us better and bolder thinkers. From Pat Stevens' expression, I doubted that she agreed. She did ask how long I'd be in town, and suggested we meet for a walk in Cheesman Park near her apartment. Sandal and Gladdie invited us to their Lookout Mountain studio to view the Amazon. Marty complimented the birthday decorations; Audrey Louise wound one of the streamers around him and he wore it out the door.

When they were gone, I felt a tremendous letdown. I wanted to hit the sheets and sleep for two days. Joel had clean-up well under way, so Audrey Louise took my hand. "Come on, I'll walk you home."

We stood by the pool, tipped our heads together out in the late-May moonlight. "Did you miss the dancing boys in jockey straps?"

"Maybe I'll have them when I'm fifty. Besides, I loved our little camp."

"High camp," I said. "But how come Marty wasn't with his lover? Other than the poetry book, he didn't talk about him at all."

"His lover died in a car accident four years ago."

"How terrible," I said, anguished for Marty. "And there's been no new love since?"

"No."

I stared into the sky, with its tapestry of blue-black swirls like portals where dreams could enter and souls commune. "Lots of loss for our friends," I sighed.

Audrey Louise put her arm around me. "Let's find Ursa the Bear."

"No, let's find the Archer. I like the idea of a womon archer in the sky." We forgot our past and searched the dots of light for the future. When she rubbed her arms and shivered, I said, "Do you remember me writing a poem about Janis Joplin?"

3
CURVE BALL

I didn't expect to find Tony taping streamers around the pool Sunday morning. "We're having a birthday barbecue lunch," he told me, twisting the crepe paper just so. Audrey Louise joined us.

"More reveling, I understand."

"Yes, the second shift. Joel insisted we invite a million neighbors and friends."

"So there's still a chance for the dancing boys."

"I just want them to eat up all that fruit."

I noticed a book on one of the poolside tables: *Beverly Gray, Star Reporter.* Published in 1940. "Whose is this?"

Tony blushed. "My bookworm son," his mom said.

"Is it any good? Maybe I should read it."

He looked as if he wished to be invisible. Then shyly he asked, "Is it hard being a reporter? Don't you get scared trying to find out things from strangers?"

"I used to. But now that makes it exciting."

"I think about becoming a writer." He tugged at the top of one of his argyles. "But I don't know what kind yet. Do you ever want to write something besides newspaper stuff?"

I almost laughed. If my beefy-armed editor at the *Beckoner* ever heard journalism called "newspaper stuff," he'd pink up like an angry rooster. "I've considered writing a novel. Maybe a mystery."

"With murder?" he asked wide-eyed.

Audrey Louise grinned. "He reads Nancy Drew."

I didn't tell him I'd seen murder close up and there was nothing fictional about it. "How about a big jewel heist instead?" I winked.

"Yeah." He winked back.

Audrey Louise sent him after iced tea, then took up her net for wanton leaves on the pool. "What were you and Pat kibitzing about in the kitchen last night?"

"I tried to extract foot from mouth about Lou Diablo. Pat made vague illusions to anti-gay sentiments."

"At the college?"

"I'm not sure. Perhaps I'll ask her today. Mind if I forgo the barbecue?"

Cheesman Park stretched out like a green palm open to dancing sun and summer-sky blue. I parked the Landry station wagon near the Roman bandshell in the middle of the park. Two reflecting pools fronted the columned, white marble enclosure. No smell of ocean in the air, but I did love the mountains and the wide tracts of grass now dotted with joggers. Pat was amenable to meeting on short notice, so long as I didn't mind her attire. "Cut-rate sweats. I run twice a day. Too much energy, I guess," she said on the phone. "And nowhere to put it."

She jogged toward me now, running with a young man. Alongside me, she pulled off a red headband and looked at her watch.

"You guessed twelve minutes. It took fourteen."

"Tomorrow," he huffed, still running in place. He looked like an inland surfer — blond, muscled, a knockout smile.

"Nyla, meet another running maniac — A.J. Farrell."

He nodded, grinning, still moving.

"I'll beat your time tonight," she told him. "But you won't be around to see it."

"Just don't push too hard in the Gauntlet." He shaded his eyes and looked toward the reflecting pools. "I see the beach bunnies are congregating. I'm outta here." He jogged down the green embankment toward the street.

"One of my students," Pat told me. "He lives two doors down."

"Who are the beach bunnies?"

She laughed. "See for yourself." She pointed toward the reflecting pools. About twenty young men splashed and strutted in skimpy bathing suits. "They call Cheesman Park 'The Beach.' Most of those guys are gay."

"And they come here to get a tan?" My turn to laugh.

"We're a long way from our college days, Nyla. How do you find your new life?"

"You mean my new life as a lesbian or now that I've discovered the materialists are in charge?"

Pat gave a wry grin. "Idealism is taking a beating these days, that's for sure." She seemed more relaxed and open. We found a sidewalk that wound past a playground and along the back of the Botanical Gardens. A wooden barricade blocked a side street that broke through that part of the park.

"That's the Gauntlet," Pat said. "Just two blocks into a cul de sac but it's all uphill. Feels like an extra two miles at the end of the run. I like the challenge."

"What about the old challenges, Pat? Politics and poetry."

She took a deep breath. Looked off into the trees. "I haven't banged the drum for years. But you know how I was. Have soapbox, will travel. I harangued and rallied and marched. With an elephant in L.A. and in San Francisco with a leatherman naked underneath his chaps. I pronounced judgement on everyone who didn't blow their closet doors off the hinges. It's a wonder D.C.C. ever hired me. I was truly a lavender menace. Then . . ." She sighed. "Lou Diablo zapped my heart like a thunderbolt and my life was never the same."

"She didn't seem like a conformist to me."

"She fought different battles than we did. She definitely wanted to fit into the system. And then work it for all it was worth, to her benefit."

"Couldn't you both have what you wanted?"

"I didn't take time to find out. I just imploded all my energy into our love affair."

We sat down on a bench. Two wimmin passed us wearing matching red running shorts. A cyclist stopped pedaling to watch the twosome, and I could smell tanning oil on her hot skin.

"We settled in," Pat said. "Bought a house. Celebrated anniversaries. Taught side by side and talked about our students. The ones with a light on inside them. The ones who had crushes on us." Her voice sounded shaky. She tapped her running shoes together, stared hard at them.

"What burst the bubble?"

"Me trying to swallow her life. I gave up my own entirely." She looked at me with tears in her eyes. "Hotspur to hausfrau."

"But why? Surely part of why she loved you was your independent spirit. And what about your writing?"

"Oh I kept writing — a poem every day for ten years. All for Lou. They weren't mine anymore."

The sun flashed off one of the reflecting pools, making the light waver like something from Merlin's wand. "Did Lou make you change? Is that why you stopped being a warrior for wimmin?"

She rubbed the edge of one eye, the way we do so as not to show our tears. "I give that impression. I know that's what Marty believes, and I've let him. I've been so bitter that she left me. But the truth is . . ." She looked me full in the face. "I can't blame Lou. She had to leave. I was suffocating her."

I touched her arm. "Why, Pat? I don't understand. Everyone who ever knew you admired you, wanted to be like you. I've recited your poetry for years. You were on the front line, showing us how to fight for justice. Showing us pride in our womonhood. You were a teacher ahead of your time."

She shook her head. "One day it all changed. I got scared."

The flames of the Wimmin's Center flickered behind my words. "What scared you that much?"

"The idea that I wasn't enough, and never could be."

Her pain bounced into me like the flash between hot wires. I knew exactly what she meant. Since a week ago when more than a building burned down. When I looked into the ashes and my lover's grieving face and wondered where to find the inspiration to keep on trying to change the world. Challenging the patriarchy by believing we could change ourselves and the lives of other wimmin for the better. Believing we could love one another amid this struggle. Now it all felt like too much to do, too few to do it, too often two steps forward and ten steps back.

"But we've traded places," Pat said then. "You're the warrior among us now."

When she touched my arm, I wanted to grab her and hold on and tell her, *I'm as scared as you are. We haven't traded places at all. We're a double image of each other.*

"I'm just glad we haven't all burned out."

"I still think of you as the hotspur poet, Pat. I'd like to see your poems for Lou."

She gave me a tired smile. "They read like a warrior turned love slave. I haven't shown them to anyone, even Marty." When our eyes met, she held mine with that same challenge I'd seen last night. And then, for a moment, I saw something else. Hope? Relief? "Maybe I could share them with you."

We walked back toward my car, and I remembered her comments in the kitchen. "Pat, last night you alluded to certain people not being comfortable about gay teachers. Has something happened at the college? Someone bugging you about being gay?"

She sighed, and put her headband back on. "Lou and I were together ten years. That's plenty of time for rumors, and for kids to gossip. We got a few phone calls — you know, heavy breather types. And some badly misspelled notes. 'Down with Q-W-E-A-R-S,' was my favorite."

"That's it? You sounded more foreboding last night."

"It's just that I worry about Marty thinking things are safe. He knows better. AIDS has everyone scared, including the liberal D.C.C. regents. When the liberals retreat, the nutsos have a field day."

I didn't buy her brushoff. "Has someone got your number?"

She offered another tired smile. "Let's just say I've got a prankster trying to get some attention. Last night someone soaped OUTLAW LEZ TEACHERS on my car window. That's why I was late, I had to clean it off. But I'm pretty sure I know who it is, and I can nip it in the bud."

I saw a quick spark in her eyes.

"In a way, it's giving my old radical heart a rev."

Pat gave me the address of a gay bookstore near Cheesman, so I went to get a copy of *White Boys in Love.* I liked the oak porch of Category Six, sitting up high off Downing Street with a huge lavender OPEN sign. Strains of Lucy Blue played as I stepped inside. A man in his mid-thirties wearing a red-flannel shirt said from behind the counter, "Hi, come on in." Another man — muscular with black hair and mustache — set a plate of nachos on a table nearby. "Snacks," he said with a grin, looking like Denver's answer to Errol Flynn. I introduced myself as a friend of Pat and Marty's, and asked about the poetry book.

"Ah, our infamous Dr. Evans," the man at the counter responded, smiling. His eyes were the blue grey of spring ice on a pond. "Our local sensation." He went to find a copy.

I browsed. Past magazine copies of *Leatherman* and *Bondage Beauties* nestled alongside *Lesbian Nuns: Breaking Silence* and *High Hearts*. What a wonder, a place where they could all live together in harmony. A full bookcase was devoted to books on AIDS — the great specter of disharmony.

Two wimmin helped themselves to nachos — both wimmin in denim, their frames lean and hard as if they'd stepped out of a cowboy commercial. At first glance I thought twins, then guessed sisters close in age. One was taller and wore a turquoise bandanna; her sister's matching scarf was wrapped around her wrist. The older sister pushed a lank of dark hair off her eyes and nodded at me.

The man returned with the book. "I'm Neal, by the way, if you need help with anything else. And please tell Marty and Pat hello."

A womon stepped in the door demanding, "You got my stack?"

I stared. She had on three layers of different dresses over sweat pants, a mashed Mets cap, red hightops, and sparkly purple disco gloves, bulging shopping bags in each hand.

Neal slid a stack of ten or twelve books toward her. She scanned them quickly. "Forty-seven bucks. With tax."

"Forty-seven oh-six," he answered, grinning. "You got a calculator mind, Mary."

She slapped the money on the counter, and scooted the books into one bag. "Numbers are safe. They can't never call you an S.O.B." She de-materialized with no goodbye.

"Takes all kinds." Neal winked.

I paid for my book and left the store smiling, the sisters watching me with faces like two closed moons.

In the car, I opened to the dedication page of *White Boys in Love.*

> "To Martin James Evans, my favorite white boy. Mentor, lover, friend, brother. Fancy dancer, explorer, horizon jumper. My hero, my poetry in motion."

Enough to make the regents choke on their croissants, all right. But sweet in a way. I headed for the highway. Wondered for a moment why Marty wasn't also a target for pranksters.

Back in Aurora, both the fruit and the guests were gone. Joel sweated over teaching Sam to throw a curve ball. Mark stood at bat, and Tony, weighed down with a huge chest protector and mask, played catcher.

"Oh for chrissakes," Joel steamed. "Just lock your elbow and follow through."

"If it's so easy, maybe you're not showing me right," Sam argued.

Mark jumped up and down. "I can do it, Dad. Let me, let me try."

Tony watched in silence as the voices rose. Finally he flung off his mask and marched up to his brother. "*Wrist*," he said, lifting Sam's arm. "Loosen it, flick it side to side, *then* lock your elbow." He took the ball and pitched a whizzer to Mark, right over the strike zone, with a clever last-minute curve outside. "Wrist," he said again to Sam.

"Elbow," Joel grumbled.

I noticed quiet amusement in Audrey Louise's eyes. Dusk's waning light signaled an end to the baseball lesson. I wondered if Pat was enjoying her run in the Gauntlet. The phone jangled inside the house. "I'm the closest, Audrey Louise. I'll get it."

I wasn't expecting Marty's voice.

"Get to Presbyterian Hospital. Pat's been hurt. And Nyla, the police think it was no accident."

4
THE LOTUS

Audrey Louise and I found Marty with two patrol officers in the Emergency Room at Presbyterian.

"Pat's been hit by a car," he told us, his eyes holding fear and anger. "And the driver didn't stick around."

"My god, how is she?" Audrey Louise asked.

"A severe concussion. Broken ribs, fractured shoulder. Some guy from the Botanical Gardens crew found her on the grassy knoll in the Gauntlet."

"What did you mean on the phone — about this being no accident?"

Marty cocked his head toward the policemen. "Their commander's around here somewhere. Said he found something in Pat's backpack. So far he hasn't said what. Just asked me a lot of questions about her running schedule."

Sandal and Gladdie appeared, like mobile tepees in their ponchos. A womon in surgery greens pushed through swinging doors from the examining rooms, and headed toward us.

"Here's Dr. Powers," Marty said. "How's Pat? Will she be all right?"

The doctor sighed and rubbed one temple. "She's still unconscious, and she isn't responding as well as I'd like. I'm running some more neurological tests. With a head injury, nothing is predictable. I think you'd better get someone from her immediate family here as soon as possible."

"Neurological tests — you mean brain damage?"

Dr. Powers couldn't have missed the panic in Marty's face. "It's possible. Let me know when her family gets here."

Brain damage — what would that mean? The thought stunned us all. Finally I said, "What about Pat's family?"

"It's just her mother, in Kansas City. I guess I'll have to call her."

"Are they close?" Sandal asked.

"As two continents." Marty's green eyes burned. "Same map, distant borders."

A.J. Farrell hailed us in the hallway. "I just heard about Pat. Some cops were talking to the apartment manager. Is she okay? Man, I should have been with her."

"They're doing neurological tests," Marty answered.

"Do you usually run together in the evening?" I asked A.J.

"Yeah. Except Sundays I meet with a Torts tutor."

Dr. Powers reappeared with a third policeman who held an orange backpack and a plastic bag, apparently Pat's clothing. They talked briefly. Then he set his sights on us.

"I'm Officer Roy Dugan, Commander of the Denver District Traffic Patrol."

We introduced ourselves, and he motioned to the other patrolmen to join us. "Let's sit down." Of A.J. he asked, "Did Pat Stevens run at the same time every evening? And did she always take the Gauntlet?"

"As far as I know."

"She ever run with anyone else but you?"

"No."

"What about the driver?" Marty insisted.

"We canvassed the park within six minutes of the call. There were only three runners. No one saw a car come out of that cul de sac. The crime lab is at the scene now, and I've got extra cruisers in the area."

"What did that guy say, the one who found her?"

"He checks the barricade on the cul de sac every night before he goes off shift. It had been moved aside, so he went to put it in place. That's when he saw the victim up on the knoll." Dugan squared his shoulders and shifted the weight of his gun belt. "She was wearing this backpack. I've examined the contents." He set the pack on the coffee table. One strap had been jerked from its anchor, the buckle bent in half. A portion of the skinned nylon held grass stains. "Did Pat Stevens tell any of you about receiving threatening notes?"

Marty's mouth sagged open. "What the —"

32

A.J. shifted restlessly, his Adidas jogging shoes making swack-swack sounds on the linoleum. Sandal lit a cigarette.

"Pat told me about some notes this morning," I said, and all eyes shifted to me. "But nothing recent. She also said someone had soaped a message on her car window last night."

"Before she came out to the house?"

I nodded at Audrey Louise.

"What was the message?" Commander Dugan asked. I felt on the spot about answering because it would reveal Pat's lifestyle. "Did she tell you?" His tone suggested he thought she had.

"Outlaw Lez Teachers."

I saw A.J.'s surprise as Marty said, "What about these notes, Commander? Apparently you found some in the backpack."

He nodded. "About ten of them." He looked at me again. "Did Ms. Stevens tell you anything else?"

"She mentioned phone calls, heavy-breather types. Again, she said this was all in the past." I hesitated, wishing Pat were here to speak for herself instead of me feeling like I was opening her life for full review. "She called this episode with the window the work of a prankster. I think she had an idea who did it."

"Did she say that exactly?" Dugan persisted.

"Yes. And that she thought she could nip it in the bud."

He opened the backpack and pulled out a slip of pink paper encased in a plastic evidence bag. "She was a little late."

From his notebook, he pulled a sheet of paper. "I made a xerox copy." I read it, passed it around our little circle. Each face reflected disbelief.

"Your bitch dumped you, and the college
    will be next.
No more gravy days for perverts, it's
    clean-up time.
Cut out the deadwood. Cut out your
    disease.
Out of the closet, into a coffin."

"Some prankster," Dugan said.

A.J. handed the xerox back to the commander. I could
see him putting two and two together, probably the
campus rumors about Pat and Louisa Diablo. Gladdie
rubbed Sandal's shoulder. Audrey Louise moved close to
Marty.

"I don't like how this shapes up," Dugan went on.
"That street blocked off, but the barricade moved. Funny
time of day too — dusk falling and the park mostly
deserted. Now these notes. After I review my prelims and
the lab report, we may bump this to Assault." He stood
up, the vinyl chair crackling, his ammo belt creaking.
"Maybe we'll get a paint sample from the clothes for a
lead on the car. I'll let you know." He started to pick up
the pack. "Oh, I won't need this." He handed Marty a
leather notebook.

Marty looked through several pages. "Her poems for
Lou." He sounded surprised. "I've never seen them."

I knew Pat had intended them for me.

We sat in silence for a few minutes after Dugan and
the other patrolmen left. Perhaps feeling the outsider or
wishing to deal with his own thoughts, A.J. exited shortly
after the policemen. Finally Marty said, "Should we try to
contact Lou?"

34

Sandal stubbed out her cigarette, mashing it to a squashed little square. She glanced at Gladdie, then answered, "She's out of the country."

"I didn't know that. Did Pat know?" His hand went to his beard. "For chrissakes, you could have told me."

Sandal didn't respond.

"Is there any way to reach her?" he asked.

"I doubt it," Sandal answered. "She only comes in from the digs on weekends."

Marty's sarcasm surprised me. "Got a girlfriend in the wilds, does she?"

"Go to hell, Martin," Sandal said with a stiff flick of her poncho.

Despite our urging, Marty wouldn't leave the hospital. "If you sit up all night, you'll be no use to Pat tomorrow," Sandal told him, but he wouldn't budge. Audrey Louise suggested he go to supper with us and then come back later.

"I've got no appetite."

"How about a brandy?" Gladdie tried. This he considered, but finally declined.

"Why don't the rest of you go home, get dinner and a decent night's sleep," I said. "You can spell us in the morning."

Gladdie agreed. "Split up the troops, send in reinforcements tomorrow — good strategy, Nyla." Sandal nodded. "All right," Audrey Louise acquiesced. "But you call if you need anything at all."

When we were alone, Marty pulled at his hair and stared at Pat's notebook. "Thanks for staying, Nyla." He tried to smile.

"Maybe now's a good time to call Pat's mother."

He looked at the notebook as if he didn't want to leave it.

"I'll stand guard," I told him. He nodded in a distracted way and wandered into the hallway.

I ran my hand down the spine of the notebook and over its covers. Turquoise flowers had been hand-tooled, a spirogyra of fine lines marking the blooms. I ran my finger around one flower, an eight-petaled lotus. *Les femmes parlent aux fleurs* — words painted underneath the lotus. Wimmin talk to flowers. And when they answer, it is poetry.

Marty returned, shaking his head.

"Wasn't she home?"

"Worse. She was." He started pacing.

"You want some coffee?"

He didn't hear me. "This seems crazy. It can't be happening. How could anyone hurt Pat? Just drive off like that. She was finally coming out of the breakup, and it's been a long haul. Especially since her dad died of cancer only two years ago. And before that . . . she never got over Stephen."

I didn't ask. I knew he would tell me.

He rubbed his eyes. Slumped down on the vinyl couch. "She always doted on her baby brother. The family came out from K.C. to celebrate his high school graduation. God, I remember that day like it was yesterday. They dragged one of those fancy Winnebagos up to Evergreen, and we all went hiking. Stephen couldn't stop babbling about college, he was so excited. Then on the third day, he went out by himself. And he never came back."

He forced a short, hard laugh. "Rose, Pat's mother, hated camping, even with the Winnebago. Every time we went out to hike, she'd call after us, 'For godssakes, don't get lost.' "

Marty stared at a spot on the wall two feet above my head, as if his eyes could carve through the sheet rock.

"They found no sign of him at all?"

"Not a trace. He simply vanished."

What an incredible burden of loss Pat had carried.

With a long sigh, Marty added, "Stephen was Rose's pride and joy. As for Pat — well, Pat was the lesbian daughter."

He pressed his hand on the notebook cover. Then pulled up his knees and turned away from me on the couch. Eventually he fell asleep.

Down one hallway, I found a sun gallery not yet locked and went out into the night air. The smell of coming rain hit me and I breathed deeply. Over the mountains, the moon burned cold through roiling clouds. Tonight it would pour down — the male rain of the Navajos that would break the flower stalks and pound on the pool in Aurora.

I took in more of the wet air, dreamed myself in that moment hand-in-hand with Lucy on our deck in Oregon. Dreamed she reached inside my shirt and touched my heart, healed our silence. Left a piece of herself as my hope, a small roaring seashell.

Back in the waiting room, Marty showed no repose in his sleep. I knew he'd wake up stiff as hell. Again I turned to the turquoise notebook and Pat's poems.

> You are my rhythmic chant
> My ancient vibration
> Opening the ocean of yourself
> With a whisper
> 'Yes, dive in here, it is safe.'

But it was not safe. Love never is.

> I feel the soft inside of your fingers,
>   the slick of your sleeve.
> Think I'll have your hand to hold forever.
> How quick the touch when you slide away,
> Gone forever.

I remembered a Buddhist story about the Sacred Lake of Lotuses. Souls of the faithful slept in the flower buds until they were called to Paradise.

5
BRICKWORK

I watched the midnight hours relax Marty's troubled face. About six-thirty, I decided to stretch my legs. On my second lap around the hospital, a red convertible screeched off the street into the entry drive and jerked to a halt at the E. Room doors. A.J. jumped out on the passenger side and grabbed a stack of books. I couldn't see the driver. A.J. said something, and the convertible sped away. He tossed an angry gesture at the retreating car.

"That looked like trouble," I observed, reaching him in the driveway.

He grinned as if I'd caught him cussing in church. "Just a few words with a frat buddy about my car. His is forever in the shop. How's Pat?"

"Nothing new. What are you doing here so early?"

He grinned again. It was part of his basic energy, too much for one person, brimming over. "Pat's got me in the habit of an early run every morning, so now I take seven-thirty classes. Thought I'd just stop here first and see if Professor Evans needed anything."

"We won't know till he wakes up," I told him, and as we went into the hospital, A.J. said, "Same for Pat, I guess."

We found Marty sopping his face with a paper towel.

"You look like some coffee might do you," A.J. offered. Marty ignored him, paced around the waiting room. "Why don't we know something by now — from the police or Dr. Powers?"

I asked A.J. to go for the coffee. "Cinnamon rolls too." I knew about starving a fever and feeding a cold. What did you do for grief?

Marty ran his hands through his hair and then checked his watch. "Hell, I need a shower. I have a class at eight-thirty, I'm meeting Rose Stevens' plane at noon. Where's she going to stay? I better get a hotel reservation."

"Won't she stay at Pat's apartment?"

"She never did before."

A.J. came back with a tray of coffee and rolls just as Dr. Powers found us, looking like she'd been up all night. "Did you contact the family?" she asked Marty.

"Yes. Her mother's flying in this morning."

Dr. Powers had gorgeous cheekbones, the kind with natural blush the color of peach blossom. Her eyes might offer a delicate fire if she was not so tired.

"It's imperative that a relative be here now. Pat Stevens has slipped into a coma."

This new blow hit us hard. Even as Dr. Powers added, "This isn't uncommon with trauma head injuries, and it could be quite short-lived. Unless it's what we call a shearing injury. That's serious, hard to diagnose, and difficult to treat. For the time being, it's wait and see." She took a deep breath, as if this kind of news never got any easier to deliver. "I hope I'll have better news later today."

We barely had time to cope with this bombshell when Commander Dugan pushed through the ER doors as if he wouldn't mind shouldering them off the hinges. His glance fell on the coffee that A.J. hadn't touched, and I handed it to him. "I've just been to the Gardens to see if any of the other crewmen were around last night. I've also got officers canvassing the high-rise on that side of the park now."

He drank half the coffee in one gulp. "Our lab guy found paint chips in her clothing. I'm still waiting on perspective photos of the cul de sac, but I went back with a measuring wheel. Just walking the distance, eyeballing the layout and where she landed, this doesn't figure."

"Are you saying it wasn't an accident?" A.J. piped up.

"I'm saying only on a longshot. Like some guy leaving his mistress, or a dope deal gone bad. The driver peels out, doesn't see her until the last minute."

"What about some kid on drugs?" Marty suggested.

"That's possible too."

"You had any robberies reported on the park?" I asked. "What about a getaway during another crime?"

42

The commander smiled. "You work with the police before?"

"Yes, I'm a newspaper reporter."

"Good instincts," he said, finishing the coffee. "We're checking everything."

"In the meantime, what's to keep the driver from getting the car repaired or painted right away?" Marty sounded angry. "And how would we know, with no identification?"

"For one thing, Dr. Evans, we got word out to radio and TV last night. Both the public and our body-shop contacts are alerted. And we'll have a color pinpointed from the paint chips by this afternoon. Make and model takes longer, but we've got a decent system. Don't forget the footwork — officers are out right now looking for witnesses." He set down the coffee cup. "One other thing works in our favor. Somewhere somebody is scared."

"Whoever wrote those notes didn't sound scared to me," Marty argued.

"Writing notes is a far cry from running someone down with a car. Unless this guy is a stone psychopath, believe me, he's plenty scared."

We'd had more than our share of bad news. I told Marty I'd call Sandal to bring him a change of clothes, and then A.J. and I would prepare Pat's apartment in case Mrs. Stevens did want to stay there. "You get her a hotel reservation so we'll have all bases covered. If you want, Audrey Louise could go with you to meet the plane."

He managed a tired smile. "I'll be fine. Just check on me this afternoon."

"You know we will."

* * * * *

43

On the drive to Pat's apartment building, I asked A.J. about his major at D.C.C.

"Pre-law. My dad's a lawyer. He and his best friend are partners. And his partner's son happens to be my best buddy, so we're following tradition." He laughed. "Robin and I thought we might get out of it and be playboys on his NFL contract. But a spinal injury scotched that."

"Why a community college for pre-law? Seems like you'd be at D.U. instead."

He laughed again. "I would've been except I let my grades slip. Like into the mud. Now I'm busting butt for straight A's so I can transfer. I'm even doing grunt work at the Capitol for the state *Law Review*." The best buddy topic seemed to be his favorite. "Robin doesn't go in for all that swords of justice stuff about the law, but he knows you can make big bucks. And it's shorter than med school."

Entering Pat's apartment, we were hit by palpable echoes of her presence — the smell of cooking from her last meal, a magazine open on the table as if she'd stopped reading to go answer the phone. I went into the kitchen just off the living room and pulled back the curtains. A.J. popped into a hallway.

"The bed's made but maybe we should change the sheets?" he suggested. "Shall I do that, or . . ."

He and Marty were alike in their sensitivity to broaching personal territories.

"I'll do it. You can do the dishes."

"Sure, no problem." He moved quickly, grabbing a towel and some dish soap. "Sheets are in the hall closet, I think. That's where I've seen her put towels." As if he didn't want me to think he paid attention to her sheets.

44

I found the sheets right where he said they were and went about my task. On the headboard, a picture frame had been turned on its face. She hadn't thrown it against a wall in anger, shattering the glass, she'd just turned it around. I looked at her with Lou arm in arm on a hill among the ruins of a temple, the Aegean burning so blue in the background it looked like wet sky. On the corner of the picture was the inscription: "1977 — Ayia Triada, Temple of Love. They built it just for us. Lou."

Pat's desk in the bedroom showed no recent fever of writing — no scattered files, no failed words wadded into little white paper balls. Everything was neatly stacked and filed. She'd hung several pictures there — one of her family, which I didn't expect for some reason. Stephen looked so like her with his dark curls, soft face, and intense black eyes. Her father looked ruddy and cheerful. Rose Steven's expression was unsmiling, guarded. No camera would ever steal her soul. There was also a small painting called "The Golden Surf," an ocean wave curling onto shore in the grey-golden aura of moonlight.

The comforter on the bed had a handmade quilted top on which mauve kites bore white stars. Pat was a kite herself. How could we reel her back to earth? "All finished," A.J. announced from the doorway, running his dishrag over Pat's bureau for good measure. Then he patted a star on one of the kites.

As always, Audrey Louise provided refuge. I found her sunning in one of the lawn chairs. She'd sent Joel off to work and the boys to morning camp. I dangled my feet in the pool and filled her in.

"Pat in a coma," she sighed. "People can stay that way for years."

"Dr. Powers said she could come out of it any time."

"Oh, I hope so. And I hope the police find that driver."

We stared at the pool, listened to it slap against its edges. Then she asked, "Did you get any sleep last night?"

"No, mostly I watched Marty. He slogged totally out, I mean, to the underworld."

"I worried about you both, so I couldn't sleep either. I read *White Boys in Love*."

"How was it?"

"The word *stud* comes up a lot."

We smiled at each other. The phone rang, and she answered it on the porch. "Hi Gladdie, what's up? Sure she's here. Just a sec." She dragged the cord out to me at the pool.

"Nyla, have you heard from Marty this afternoon?"

"Not yet. I plan to call him pretty soon."

"Good. I've got such an odd feeling about him. Ever since we read the xerox of that pink note, I've been hearing an old rhyme over and over in my head. 'Sticks and stones can break my bones, but words can never hurt me.' Probably just psychic static. But I'd appreciate a call after you talk to him."

I thought about Dugan's comment. "I always trust good instincts, Gladdie. Thanks for letting me know."

Audrey Louise suggested I invite Marty for dinner, since this was family bowling night. "I've even got the steaks and wine."

With the charcoal smoking nicely and the white zin on ice, I went onto the deck to watch the sunset. The yard was incredibly quiet. Wind blew over the pool and stirred the tops of the tulips. I heard a windchime in the eaves.

Loving is a passage, I thought, and Pat's poems had shown me that part of love is loss. Ten years with Lou, then desolation of the soul. Would I have ten years with Lucy? I asked the fading sun. What did Lou feel? I asked the tulips.

When Marty trudged up the stairs about seven-thirty, I said, "You look like hell."

"I *feel* like hell."

"Any change?"

He shook his head. I offered him wine as he stretched out on the couch. He plopped his shoes on the floor, and sighed. "God, Nyla, I appreciate this."

He reported successfully ferrying Rose Stevens from the airport to the hospital. "She won't stay at Pat's apartment. She's in a hotel near Presbyterian. You wasted the cleanup job."

"A.J. made it fast. He really cares about Pat. Even with the revelation from the notes."

"So he should be sainted?"

I would never get used to Marty's quick sarcasm — our guru's critical flaw. "Not at all. But for some people, finding out a friend is gay ends the friendship."

He sighed and stretched. "Pat says he's a big frat man, hangs out with the jocks." He stared into his wine glass. "This was Ronnie's favorite time of the evening. Changing of the guard, he called it."

"Tell me about him."

He smiled. "He was gorgeous — lithe and honey-blond, walked on his toes like a dancer. Much younger than I, and he had a past. I didn't care. I would have followed him anywhere." He toasted twilight, finished his wine, and got up to pour himself another glass. "One day we were together. The next day he was

47

gone, and I never got the chance to say goodbye. I was furious for years."

He drank half of the new glass of wine in one swallow. "Odd, isn't it, how love gets tangled up with so much anger. Pat's never wanted to admit that about her breakup with Lou. So she's just bounced around, numb and confused, between anger and grief." He drank the rest of the wine and poured himself yet another. "I know all about that."

He looked out the deck doors. "They had something, that fire between them. The one you hope will never burn out. I figured if *they* had it, maybe I could find it again."

He chugged the wine. I could see he was well on his way to drowning his sorrows, and I couldn't blame him.

"I wondered if you weren't gay in college," he teased. "Even when I heard you were getting married. Hell, I never saw the guy — you were always with Audrey Louise."

"That should have told me something," I said. "Marty, when Stephen disappeared, how long did the search go on?"

He sobered immediately. "Days. Weeks. They tried everything. Special mountain patrol, private investigators, ChildFind — you name it. There were posters up everywhere, but it was like he dropped off the face of the earth."

He made his way back to the couch. "Damnedest thing is, I was the last to see him. He came over from their campsite to my cabin. Just like in the movies, a beautiful child on my doorstep." He laughed to himself. "I gave him a beer — trying to treat him like a college man, you know. And we sat there talking for hours. We never got to talk like that before, his family was always around. Hell, I couldn't take my eyes off him. The sunlight on his

48

forehead, the soft curl of his hair on his neck. Grey eyes like . . . like . . ." He sighed loudly. "I'll never forget him walking back down to the trail. He turned to me and raised his hand, called 'So long, pal,' like he had the whole rest of his life ahead of him."

He rubbed his head as if to wake himself up. "I suppose Pat thought the same thing when she went out for her run yesterday."

"She never told you about the notes or the phone calls?"

He shook his head. "She can be very private. Can I have some more wine?"

"Only if you agree to spend the night."

"Ms. Wade, what of my reputation?"

"It will survive."

"All right, but I left Pat's notebook in my car and I want to bring it in. That's the first thing she'll ask for when she . . ."

He got that panicked look again. I hugged him. "Pull up into the driveway while you're at it."

I went out onto the deck, welcoming the cool air. I heard his feet crunch below in the gravel. I'd have to call Gladdie and let her know he was safe and sound. Clouds across the moon reminded me of Oregon. His headlights flicked on. The VW engine turned over. Then I heard the roar of another car, a screech of tires, a crash, and shattering glass. Marty's Volkswagen jumped the curb, bumped over the gravel of the driveway, and crashed through a length of picket fence heading straight for the swimming pool.

I took the stairs two at a time and ran out into the dark backyard. Sure I'd find the Bug bubbling toward the bottom of the pool. But Marty had jerked the steering wheel just in time. The car swacked sideways against a

49

sturdy elm. There it sat, its windshield broken out, the hood popped and bent.

Marty scrambled out the door, holding his hand over one eye. Blood gushed through his fingers. I reached for him, but he batted my hand away and turned angrily back to the car where he groped around on the floorboard. He picked something up, and we both stared at it: a red brick painted with pink letters. FAG BUSTERS.

6
ON THE PROWL

The noise of the crash woke up the whole neighborhood. An Aurora patrolman made the scene within five minutes, but everything had happened too fast. Marty didn't get a good look at the car — nor did I — or at the driver who hurled the brickbomb.

The patrolman questioned the neighbors, but turned up nothing. We showed him the brick. "Some bad joke," he said.

Porter Memorial was only six blocks from the house. We got there fast enough to wait an hour for a doctor to stitch Marty's eye.

"There was no other car on the street, Nyla," he said while we waited. "The driver came at me with his lights off."

"Like he waited in ambush."

"Guess Pat's attacker has added me to his list."

He came out of the examining room looking weak-kneed and wearing a cockeyed gauze patch over his left eyebrow. I drove him back to the apartment. We'd call a wrecker in the morning. The Landrys were home by then, the boys crawling over, under, and around the Beetle so awkwardly coupled with the elm. "We'll sort it all out in the morning," Audrey Louise declared, weary and worried.

Marty zonked out as soon as I pulled a blanket over him. Shock and pain-killers. I stared at the starlight coming in my window. *Sticks and stones will break my bones* . . . Gladdie's instinct had been right on target. And so had the brick.

I slept fitfully, and at daybreak went for a walk. I used the phone on the back porch of the main house to call Sandal's studio. Gladdie answered. I told her what happened. "I fear this isn't their last visit," she said.

Marty was awake when I returned to the apartment. He looked bleary-eyed, with most of the left side of his face mottled purple and green. I suggested he cancel his classes, but he chose perseverance and a pain pill. Holding his hand over the patch above his eye, he dressed slowly. Called the hospital to check on Pat. The head nurse reported no change. We could have used better news.

"Leave you two alone and you drive a car through my fence," Audrey Louise chided. We stood by the pool and

53

watched the wrecker rig drag the battered VW away. We examined the brick again; I told her I was headed to see Commander Dugan.

Clearly, the city of Denver didn't spend one dime on decor in the police building. Commander Dugan was surrounded by the paperwork of a thousand traffic cases. "Welcome to the bullpen," he said, and pointed to the coffee pot across the room. "Help yourself."

I showed him the brick and told him what happened. He hefted it from hand to hand. "Stone of retribution?"

"I can't believe this is just unlucky coincidence."

"No," he agreed. "I've been studying the perspective photos." He opened a folder. "You been on traffic cases as long as I have, you start to see skid patterns in your dreams. Wake up your wife with velocity numbers instead of sweet nothings."

He frowned. "We've got both skids and scuffs on this case." He showed me several of the photographs, as well as his triangulation measurements to determine point of impact. "Good math and guesswork," he said. "And luck, don't forget luck." He pointed to one photograph. "A fertilizer spreader drove into the cul de sac that day after the rain. So we had some extra surface. That was our luck.

"Here's the scuff — a friction mark made by a slipping or rotating tire, usually when a car speeds up." Next we looked at two short, dark tire skids. "You get skids with a locked wheel, when a driver hits the brakes."

His calculations were full of scratchouts. "I worked back from the photos and measurements taken on-site to figure out velocity. With acceleration at the scuff mark and braking at the skid mark." He showed me a diagram.

"This vehicle had to rev up hard on a mighty short leash."

He tapped one thick finger on the skid photo. "Lots of tread-mark. Tires under-inflated. Add that to the under-body rust we found in the street and the paint samples. Look at the distance she was thrown. My guess is this is an old car, probably fat as a tank."

"Your lab get anything conclusive from the paint?"

Dugan smiled. "It's hospital green, that pukey color that makes you want to get well soon. It doesn't match any of our color samples back to nineteen-seventy-four. The FBI has samples from day one . . ." He headed for the coffee pot. "But that's a six week wait easy. I know some garage guys. They can give us an estimate on the year lots quicker."

"No leads on a witness, then?"

He shook his head. "But we're still pounding the pavement. Three residences flank the cul de sac. One family's on vacation, no one at home at the other, and the lady at the third house didn't see or hear anything." He smiled into his coffee. " 'Course I got the feeling she wouldn't have lifted the shade if she *had* heard anything."

"Why not?"

"The comments she made about what goes on in the park. Said she wasn't surprised there was trouble. Runners aren't supposed to be in the cul de sac, and apparently they aren't the only people who wander up there for privacy."

"You mean she's seen some of the Cheesman beach boys?"

He nodded. "Parks patrol is questioning runners and sunbathers, just in case we missed somebody."

"Are you ready to move the case to Assault?"

"Leaving the scene doesn't prove intent, but these tire marks could. I'm meeting with their chief of detectives this afternoon. In the meantime, I had the lab check all the notes for prints. Nothing. I even scanned the PDID reports — Public Disorder Intelligence Division. To see if any recent harassment incidents had a similar m.o." He leaned back in his chair. "What paper do you work for?"

"The *Beckoner* in Burnton, Oregon. My editor calls it a three-hick paper in a three-hick town, but we cover our share of felonies."

"You might use your news nose to help us. Check with the Gay and Lesbian Community Center," Dugan suggested. "They get harassment reported to them that we never see. Maybe something's heating up."

The commander loaned me his phone for the call to the *Beckoner* offices. "Vacation not all it's cracked up to be?" Gruff Hamilton gloated. I envisioned him with a blue pencil behind one ear and a cigarette behind the other. Glasses pushed up into his crewcut. None of his shirts had known an iron in years. I gave him a quick review of events. "I think I can help if you give me a local press contact."

He muttered vague protest while he checked his files. "Sticking your neck out again . . . you're like a damned bulldog . . ." Lucy had told me that my chase after justice would eventually turn Gruff's Navy tatoos pale. Finally he said, "Eleanor Bead. City News Bureau."

The City News Bureau served as a local UPI, set up to scoop the Denver dailies. A place for cub reporters to earn their stripes. High tension for low pay. The chief editor offered me a one-volt handshake. "Call me Bead."

Certainly Eleanor seemed too soft. I judged her about forty — tall with jet black hair and the perfect shoulders for designer coats. But her eyes were set too close together and she walked in her heels like her feet longed for cowboy boots. She'd run the bureau for five years.

I asked if she'd heard about the hit-and-run. She fussed with some folders. "Professor at the college, right?" I told her about the threatening notes and the brick-bomb.

"Sounds juicy. Homophobia Berserka."

I didn't like the glint in her eye. "Pat Stevens is in a coma and Marty Evans nearly got his brains bashed in."

"Yes, yes, of course, but it's still great copy." She poked at her files again, then ran her ferret eyes over me. "You think there's a neo-Nazi queer-monger squad lurking about the D.C.C. campus?"

"If there is, I want to find out."

She stared at me like Sister X-Ray snooping out my soul. "I'll get you a press pass. You get me the good dirt."

I drove to Category Six to ask Neal for the name of the GLCC director. Mused about Dugan taking the gay issue in stride, while Bead spied it as grist for a scoop.

Neal stood in the doorway with his Errol Flynn cohort, who had just removed the entire door lock and handle.

"How's Pat?" Neal asked. "We heard about her on the radio."

"Still in a coma. And they haven't located the driver or the car that hit her."

He shook his head.

57

"What's with the door lock?"

"Someone poured glue in it so we had to break a window to get in this morning. Lucky you're so handy with tools, Dan." He patted his partner's shoulder.

"This isn't the first time," Dan told me. "But we didn't expect a calling card." He handed me a bright pink flyer. A crude pine tree had been drawn on it with block letters underneath.

"Qwears can't see the forest for the trees.
But the Sons of God have clear vision.
We find what's rotten and cut out the
deadwood.
It's clean-up time for decent society.
Time for the work of the Foresters."

"Nelly paper for such a Republican protest," Neal said.

"You ever hear of this group?"

"No. You think they might be an auxiliary to Woodmen of the World?"

Dan laughed.

Cut out the deadwood. Clean-up time. The misspelling of the word Qwears. All similar to the notes Pat had received. So Gladdie was right again, there had been another visit. I told them what had happened to Marty.

"Someone's definitely on the prowl," Neal said.

7

FOREST FOR THE TREES

I found the Gay and Lesbian Community Center housed in a Unitarian church. The director, Gene Nile, was affable even after years of struggle for funding, volunteers, and a lasting peace for Denver's gay community.

"When we started out, we couldn't pay the phone bill. Now we have two full-time staffers."

I thought, *We had our own building, and now we have a cornerstone.* Then chided myself for wishing company in misfortune. I told him about the assault on Pat, the brick-bashing, and the ensuing harassment at the bookstore. I showed him the Forester flyer.

"Something familiar in this. We certainly get our share of threats." He located a file marked GET OUTTA TOWN QUICK.

I would have laughed except there was no humor in the contents. A lengthy harangue from a Baptist minister, obscene sketches, and garish anti-gay cartoons. Even a threat made with words cut out of a newspaper. "I speak to God. And He has marked you for a dark eternity."

Gene smiled. "Dark eternity, I kinda liked that. Sounds like a good mystery title." He glanced at me. "Don't get me wrong. There's nothing funny in these threats. But you have to keep a sense of humor."

At the back of the folder I found another pink sheet of paper. It matched the Forester flyer.

"I thought I recognized that pink protest," Gene said. He unclipped several newspaper articles in the folder.

"In May of eighty-six, someone vandalized a gay doctor's house. Painted FAGGOT BOY LOVER in a red splash four feet tall across the front porch. And skewered these flyers on the metal pickets of his security fence."

Apparently the Forester story didn't end in the splash of red paint. "Here's another article. My column for *Out Proud*." He quickly reread it. "At the same time, flyers also appeared at the Colorado Board of Nursing Review with a gay male nurse's name written on the back. And one showed up at the Denver district Board of Education with a lesbian teacher's name on it. The accusation is enough to make everybody involved very uncomfortable."

"No press generated in the dailies?"

"Not that I know of. And I certainly didn't mention any names."

"I'm convinced the incidents involve someone at D.C.C. But things have obviously escalated. From red paint and pink flyers to this violence."

"The AIDS scare is making everything worse. Nationally, violence is up by fifty percent. Locally, we're getting more reports all the time — people cruising the bars and throwing beer bottles, cars broken into, fistfights."

"I read about a case in *The Advocate*," I said. "At least those people were convicted."

"Most of the time they're not." Gene sighed. "Most of the time nothing is even reported. People are too afraid of the publicity."

"What about the Denver police? The traffic commander seems copasetic."

"We have a commissioner busy with other problems right now. It hasn't always been that way. The attitude at the top trickles down to patrol. They bounce between ignoring us and being too interested."

"How do these gaybashers find the bars?"

Gene shrugged. "People call here for addresses. Or read *Out Proud*. Our visibility is hard-earned, but it still has a price."

The smell of freshly-baked oatmeal cookies wafted through Audrey Louise's house. I found her in the kitchen baking and munching. Joel and the boys were out fixing the fence. We watched from the window — Mark trying to hold the posthole digger while Sam jumped on it to drive it into the ground. Tony fastidiously stirred a can of white paint. Joel had stripped off his shirt to ferry the dirt in a wheelbarrow out to the alley.

Audrey Louise said, "He'll be nursing his sacro for days."

"It's better if you don't watch." I told her about my day's visits. She stirred the cookie dough with new energy. "I can't imagine what it must feel like to sit on the carpet with a cup of coffee and the Sunday paper, scissoring it into a hate note."

"Pat Stevens knows what it feels like to read such a note." I'd been gay for three years but had just learned the meaning of perversion: don't flaunt love, flaunt violence instead.

"Straight mentality isn't very live-and-let-live, is it?" Audrey Louise said.

I shook my head. "More like mob rule."

During dinner, Marty called for relief troops. Audrey Louise and I met him at the hospital about seven. He looked beat. Told us that Rose Stevens was talking with Dr. Powers. "Pat's vitals are stable. That's all I know."

"Does your eye hurt as bad as it looks?" Audrey Louise asked. The swelling was down but a blue-black bruise mapped across his forehead.

"It hurts a lot."

"Did Mrs. Stevens ask about it?" He nodded at me. "What did you tell her?"

"That a stranger brick-bashed me for being gay."

"How did she take it?"

"Nerves of steel."

We walked to the sun gallery. I wished I could tell Marty that Dugan had found a witness. Or the driver. Instead I told him the Assault Division would probably be on the case by morning. Told him coincidence might link the Fag Busters, Sons of God, and the Foresters.

"Sounds too right-wing organized to be students," he grumped.

"But someone knows your movements, and that centers you and Pat back at D.C.C.," I countered. "And the wording and misspelling in the notes is so similar."

"Maybe it's one of the other professors," Audrey Louise suggested.

"Old grudges long harbored?" Marty considered. "No. If there was any secret in-fighting about Pat, I'd have heard it."

"Really?" I said. "Those liberal peers who make jokes about Ronnie's book would let you in on problems with Pat? Surely they knew the rumors about her and Lou as well as the students did. Two gay teachers in their midst — one might be manageable, but more than one, some people get nervous."

Marty shook his head. "No way. The whole act is too crude. We may well have homophobes among the ranks, but I don't buy them acting it out with such violence."

A womon with silver-grey hair and a commanding presence stepped into the gallery. She took in everything with her eyes, assessing all the boundaries at once.

Marty turned to her. "Rose, let me introduce you."

She was neither the guarded soul from Pat's family portrait nor the severe personality Marty had described. She was in fact grand and attractive, possessing an aura of elegance and reserve.

As Marty asked about the latest from Dr. Powers, Rose moved to a chair. "They're checking everything thoroughly," she said. "X-rays, IV. The nurses are very attentive, they rub her hands and feet, they turned her in the bed several times today. She seems to be in some pain from her shoulder. Dr. Powers expects a spontaneous recovery."

"Can we see her?" Audrey Louise asked.

"I'd like to," I said.

"She doesn't move," Rose answered, massaging her forehead.

Marty touched his bandage. "I'll leave you to it then, ladies. I need sleep."

Audrey Louise invited him to stay at the house and skip the drive up to Evergreen, but he declined. "Nothing like your own bed. I'll be out the minute I hit the pillows."

As we went into Pat's room, Audrey Louise said to Rose, "I'm sure what's happened to Pat has been an incredible shock for you."

"The three of us were in a writing group together in college," I added. "We just found each other again a few days ago."

"So there's been a shock for you too," Rose said softly.

We stood by the bed, staring at Pat. The Amazon asleep — she already looked smaller. I listened to the monitor blip, and to the loud silence. Felt Audrey Louise tense beside me.

"They say patients in a coma can hear voices," Rose said. "The nurses told me to talk to her." She shook her head in a brisk little movement that reminded me of her daughter.

Suddenly Pat rolled her head to one side and then back. Stiffened one shoulder and groaned. Audrey Louise jumped. I moved closer to the bed. Rose touched Pat, leaned toward her and spoke softly. "Pat, can you hear me? It's Mother. Can you hear me?"

Pat shuddered, and drew one hand up sharply over her eyes. In a voice that surged up from her soul, she cried out, "Lou!"

* * * * *

64

Some hours later, as I stood on the deck in Aurora, I could still hear the reverberation of Pat's monitors going off like a three-alarm fire. She scared hell out of us, and the med team quickly shuttled us out of the room. Within minutes, Dr. Powers was able to assure us that there was no crisis. Patients in a coma often cry out, even seem to awaken, without actually regaining consciousness. The sudden surge in pulse rate and temperature had set off the monitors. Despite the medical rationale, Rose looked pale and trembly when we escorted her to the hotel.

Now I wanted to write. Write something Bead could sink her teeth into. But the facts were too sparse. I could attest to Dugan's dedication, but Bead wouldn't glance twice at that. I could hint at "a related incident in Aurora." But it all added up to investigation pending, just teaser copy. That's when the phone rang.

Commander Dugan sounded mighty chipper for a cop facing night shift. "Just wanted to let you know, Ms. Wade, you'll be working with Sergeant Salvador Compoz in the Assault Division. I told him you'd be around to introduce yourself. I'm going down to LaJunta tomorrow. Special body shop contact. Maybe he can identify our paint sample. He's come up with a ringer before."

"Let's hope so. And thanks for all your help."

Restless twilight clouds, thick and grey as cannon smoke, clung to the black mountains. The moon backlit the battle clouds; they would burn into a red-fire night. "Strange brew in the heavens," I said aloud, wishing I could draw my fingertips across Lucy's cheek. I considered calling Gladdie to ask if her psychic insights led to LaJunta. Wished I felt any insight myself, not just a nagging, aching pessimism that I couldn't turn one helpful stone.

I fell asleep before ten, into dreams where Pat cried out and Rose fell back stricken, the ghost of Lou flying up between them. I floundered in love lost, love missed, and so much fear of loving. Floated inside a barrel of pink flyers. Kept seeing the face of Louisa Diablo.

Night had swallowed the moon when I awakened. I felt an echo of presence in the darkness, like a message delivered. And then running footsteps on the stairs, and pounding on the apartment door. "Let me in, Nyla, my god, let me in."

The sob in Marty's voice chilled me. "Is it Pat?"

He nearly fell into the room. "No, not Pat."

"What's wrong?"

"They know my phone number. They called me tonight."

"What did they say?"

The small force in his voice failed. " 'Get eyes in your back, faggot. You're next.' "

8

ONE–ON–ONE

We spent the hours till daylight over bourbon and coffee. "So much for my safe niche," Marty said at one point, staring out the deck doors. "It's so dark in the mountains, with the trees up close to the house. Like someone shut off the moon with a private switch." He drank the last of a cold cup. "I don't want them to run me out of my house."

"You're isolated up there. What if next time they don't call first? I want you to get some clothes and stay here a few days. Till the police have a handle on this."

"I'm already packed."

Sergeant Salvador Compoz met with us at nine a.m. I liked his looks. Straight and gaunt with chiseled cheekbones and sultry eyes. Those eyes welcomed me, as did the mint green of his shirt, cool as the underside of a lily pad. He wore a brown vintage tie streaked with yellow and silver, as if a sleek fish sunned on his chest. The buckle of his cowboy belt sported a picture agate. If he was rushed with a caseload of bail jumpers, he didn't show it. I introduced myself and Marty.

"How's the eye?"

"Looks better than it feels."

I told the sergeant about Marty's phone threat.

"You sure it was a man's voice?"

He nodded.

"You get any idea of age, accent, anything unusual?"

"No, he said it too fast. All I heard were the words." Marty held the sergeant's eyes a moment.

Compoz sat on the edge of his desk. "I've reviewed the case file. I agree with Roy Dugan's conclusions. But as you know, we have no lead on the vehicle or the driver. And no hard evidence to link the notes to the brick-bomb."

"Or to this." I showed him the Forester flyer, filled him in on what I'd learned at Category Six and the GLCC.

"Time to look for the common denominator," he concluded.

"Meaning what?" Marty asked.

"Someone with a motive, someone who views you and Pat Stevens as a threat. Probably within your own circle of friends. Or an acquaintance connected to that circle. Nine times out of ten that's where we find our perp."

"We've discussed the obvious connection to the college," I offered. "But Marty's convinced no one on the staff could be involved."

"Students, then?"

Marty didn't answer the sergeant's question, just worked his jaw muscle. I guessed he felt pretty invaded. Suddenly no place was safe — not work, home, or among friends.

"I got the impression Pat thought it might be students," I told Compoz, and repeated what she'd told me about the prankster.

"We'll look into that. And in the meantime, our division will keep working with the parks patrol questioning runners and any of the park regulars. I understand you're working with City News Bureau on this, Nyla."

Compoz had done his homework. I liked that as much as his friendly tie.

"Please include my name and contact number in any article. We often get tips that way."

"Will you give me an exclusive?"

He was caught off guard, but smiled. "You know anyone from the press can get offense reports. But I'll try to give you first crack."

"Could I use the skid photo?"

Again he smiled. "I don't want to do anything that would compromise evidence. But I'll tell you there's a point of interest on the brick. Our lab tech found an unusual mark on it. Actually looks like two letters, K and L. He's working on it now."

The sergeant stood up, squared his shoulders. "As for the phone threats, chances are this guy will call again.

Long as he's calling, he isn't acting. That buys us some time. Would you consider a phone trap, Dr. Evans? It will provide a computer listing of all incoming calls."

"Marty's staying at my apartment."

Compoz held my eyes. "I'll alert Aurora patrol." Then he looked at Marty. "We'll put the trap on that number. If the guy calls you there, that tells us he knows your movements to a tee."

No false reassurance from Compoz. No easy reality for Marty. "Guess I just show up for class like usual?" He tugged at his pony tail.

"Safety in numbers," I said.

He shook his head, looked into me for help. We all needed an Amazon.

I hopped the Number Forty bus, heading for Presbyterian. The seat back in front of me had been carved into with a knife like so much hard chocolate. *Emmanuel plus Lisa forever. Bonzo loves Karen.* Nothing is ever so simple, I thought, as love-plus-love forever. If it were, we could all escape our doubts. Pat with her soul in limbo, still longing for Lou. Marty walking around half-numbed by Ronnie's absence, and Rose Stevens wondering about so much loss in her life. Me, wondering how Lucy and I could come to terms. On a grander scale, I thought, if we could all love each other better, or even meet halfway, we wouldn't have to search among the people we thought we could trust for a common denominator to crime.

Though I didn't know most of Pat and Marty's friends, I found it hard to imagine someone in their circle capable of threats and violence. "Could be an acquaintance connected to that circle," Compoz had said. I realized I did know someone who didn't quite fit any category — A.J. Farrell. He was Pat's former student, and now her running partner. Lived in her apartment building. He seemed to be her friend. And he was Marty's acquaintance at D.C.C. Maybe he could give us a clue.

Rose wasn't in the waiting room. I headed for the cafeteria. Spotted Sandal in her bright poncho, talking intently with Rose. What did they discuss — existentialism and free form sculpture? Maybe.

Sandal hugged me. "I was telling Rose about the Passionate Few. And our warriors of the word — you and Pat."

"You've had to endure some risks in your work," Rose said. I heard something behind her words — judgement, or a question. As if she would not choose such risks. Suddenly they all seemed worth it to me.

"I learned that from Pat. She took a risk with every poem."

We talked about the Pat of college days, feeling more comfortable with those memories. Finally Rose asked, "Is she still friends with Louisa?"

I thought of their picture turned on its face. "It's been a tough year for Pat," Sandal answered.

Rose didn't ask anything more. We seemed to have run out of comfortable conversation. "I appreciate your being here," Rose said. "Both of you. But I think you should go on about your day. All there is to do is wait, and I'm used to that."

Once outside, Sandal suggested a change of scenery. I asked her to drive me to Pat's apartment. On the way, I told her about Marty's phone threat. "We've been to the police, and he's moving in with me for a while."

"This isn't the way our lives were supposed to turn out."

She ran one hand through her blonde hair, reminding me of that sunburned college girl I'd known, on the same quest to understand an imperfect world.

"Did you expect to be with Gladdie? Or was that a surprise?"

With her smile, the mood lifted. "Someone told me there was a womon playing saxophone for tips at the Student Union. So I went to see for myself. And there was Gladdie, like a life sculpture — big feet and hands, big breasts, a womon with hips and proud of them. Nothing in her afraid of her bigness, her aliveness. She could make you swoon with that honey horn of hers, or get you doing a glad-foot hop in front of total strangers. I watched her every day for a week."

We laughed. Sandal blushed. "Then we both showed up at the psychic channeling. Gladdie walked up to me and said, 'I've been in your dreams.' Hell, I was in love.

"She started driving the truck for me when I picked up stone, and helped me make clay. Elbow-deep in the squishy red of it and laughing like she was born to mix mud. Some nights she'd play her sax for me at the studio. Then she just wasn't anywhere else but with me, and I found a new richness in my work. Now we're just a couple of dotty ole broads up on our six acres." She grinned and blushed again.

"Your little corner of Paradise."

"Nothing but quality time. And just in case we get invaders . . ." She winked. "Gladdie keeps a gun full of birdshot." Then she asked, "So what's up at Pat's apartment?"

"I want to talk to her jogging partner. See if he knows anything. Even something he thinks isn't important."

Luck was with us — we found A.J. Farrell washing his red convertible out in front of the sixplex.

"That's some car you've got there," Sandal remarked. "Fifty-seven Merc, isn't it?"

A.J. flexed his tan, sweaty chest. "How'd you know the year?"

"My dad was a Merc dealer."

"This is a Turnpike Cruiser."

"Does the rev counter still work?"

For the next half hour, I watched them purr over the convertible, extolling its virtues: Merc-O-Matic pushbutton transmission, Seat-O-Matic with forty-nine positions, electric roof, dual headlamps under sharp hoods. "Kidney cutters," A.J. informed me, running his hand over the smooth metal. "Two hundred ninety horsepower when she was new," he bragged, wiping the car lovingly with his chamois. He inspected the paint near one tire, then squinted up at us. "Robin has an old Imperial. Now that's a car. A real dragon machine."

He rolled the term in his throat with admiration. "Original chrome grille, and fins out to here. But it needs a paint job and work on the interior. He says he's too busy. With monkey business, I say."

There was obvious fondness in his voice. He offered us a beer, just as another car screeched up to the curb. The driver honked and one passenger jumped out.

"Yo, A.J.," the man called as the car sped away. From the tight jeans and athlete's butt-high saunter, I guessed this must be Robin.

"Yo, Robin," A.J. answered, and they slapped a high-five.

"Ladies," he bowed to us. "The pleasure is all mine. I'm Robin Gaither." He pushed his sunglasses up into thick, sandy-blond hair. To A.J. he said, "Two at a time, bud, that's selfish."

A.J. threw the chamois at him. "I'm about to crack some Silver Bullet. Guess I don't have to ask if you want any."

Robin played Mr. Manners while A.J. made the beer run. "Sandal Morgan — aren't you the famous alum sculptor? Creator of those ravishing stone beauties at D.C.C.?"

"The same."

"They're big." He grinned.

Sandal got an ornery gleam in her eye. "Built to pull up a stiff oak by its roots."

He ignored her allusion. "Got anything new in the works?"

One of the back doors banged, and A.J. rejoined us, juggling the beer cans.

"I'm sculpting an Amazon," Sandal told them. "Future ruler of the Universe."

Robin quickly swigged his beer. Sandal's eyes fairly shone. A.J. said, "Flanks, I hope you're giving her flanks to die for." We all laughed. Especially Robin.

"An Amazon is just what Pat needs right now," I commented.

"Terrible, this accident," Robin said. "Have the cops come up with anything?"

"Not yet."

"She's a good teacher," he added. "I had her for Sophomore Comp."

"More like she had you," A.J. teased. "To put up with."

I asked to use A.J.'s bathroom. He and Robin went into the apartment with me for more beer. As I admired the grey and mauve color scheme in his towels, I heard a can hit the floor in the other room.

"For chrissakes, Robin, don't spray beer in here. This isn't the frat house."

"Just give me the car."

"I told you, I have plans tomorrow night. If you'd get the Imperial fixed, you'd have your own wheels."

"Fix the Imperial, fix the Imperial. You're a gawdamned broken record."

"What's with you, Robin? You're edgy as hell. Kay miss her period again?"

"You could do a lot worse than Kay, bud. But everyone knows you don't do diddley with anyone."

One of them tromped out, banging the screen door. Then the other one followed, popping a beer tab.

I walked through A.J.'s apartment. The rose color scheme continued in plush carpeting to the living room. In front of a grey leather couch and matching chair, there was a smokey glass-topped coffee table. Definitely not where frat boys propped their feet. In his bedroom, brass lamps with silk shades sat on art deco laquerware and an expensive Indian rug. The boy had class. I noticed several photos on the dresser. One of Robin with his perfect windblown hair, and another of them both in tuxedos with a girl in a green gown.

When I went back outside, Sandal and A.J. were leaning under the hood of the Turnpike Cruiser. Robin was gone. "Bused it back to the TKE house," A.J. said.

"Did everyone like Pat Stevens for a teacher as much as Robin did?" I asked him. "I mean, your other frat brothers?"

"Sure. She's a good citizen. Gives you a break with an overdue paper, offers makeup tests."

"So you've never heard any complaints?"

"Nope."

"What about Dr. Evans? Is he as popular?" Sandal asked.

A.J. closed the hood and gave the front of it a quick swipe with the chamois. "He's tougher. Especially on his deadlines. But I think he's fair."

I considered being diplomatic, but opted for directness. "What about their being gay? Anyone think that was worth some fun?"

Sandal raised her eyebrows at me. Both of us waited for A.J.'s answer. He ran his rag in a small circle on a spot near one headlight, then looked directly at me. "Don't know that anyone figured they were. Denver's big enough, people can have whatever private lives they want." He stared at the perfect red paint job on the car, as if it was the most important thing on his mind.

"You never heard any of the campus rumors?" I persisted.

He shook his head. "I never heard anything until this week at the hospital. When Pat first moved in here, I thought about asking her out. I wasn't her student anymore. But I figured she'd think I was too young. Now I'm glad I didn't ask her."

I thought about him calling the gay men at Cheesman beach bunnies. Wondered now why Pat hadn't questioned that remark. "What about the Gauntlet — did you usually see other runners up there? Any of the beach bunnies?"

He stretched and touched his toes. "I can't remember anyone else taking that route. It's supposed to be off limits. That's one reason we liked it so much — our last private challenge of the day." As he straightened up he added, "As for the bunnies, I don't think they run on the regular track. And certainly not in the Gauntlet."

He seemed to be exactly what he was — Pat's running partner, their friendship limited to that pursuit. "She didn't ever mention the notes then, the recent ones?"

"Heck no. I would have watched out for her."

"No change in her mood lately that you noticed?" Sandal asked.

He shaded his eyes. "We ran together, but we didn't hang out together, you know? She was, oh, always real private. Didn't talk about her feelings or her personal life." He grinned. "Unless it was sore calf muscles, or our time on the run."

Sandal invited him to take a joy ride out to see her Amazon, and we left him with his red convertible — rubbing his naked chest up against the hot, wet metal and touching it through the chamois like a lover.

She took me to lunch at Patience and Sarah's, a gay coffeehouse, where we sat under the huge poster faces of Emma Goldman and Bessie Smith. Specialty of the house was a delicious chocolate cake in the shape of a sweet Nubian breast.

"How much of Denver I never knew," I said to Sandal. She laughed. "In your other life."

Back in Aurora, I found a note from Audrey Louise. *Took the boys to see a giant electric coil create indoor lightning bolts. Hope we get a charge out of it. See you later.*

Nice to have the place all to myself. I sunned by the pool till my skin was hot, then dove in, held my breath, and pulled the weight of my body through the soundless water. Loved the odd joy of moving in this wet, heavy silence. I remembered my dream about Lou Diablo and all those floating pink flyers. But whatever message she'd sent flowed over me like the water.

I was still toweling my hair when Sergeant Compoz drove his beige Caprice up the drive. His tie hung loose at his open collar. His dark hair glistened in the sun.

"You look like you could use a dip in the pool."

He smiled, his eyes nearly the color of the water. "Looks inviting all right. Is it okay for an installer and one of my detectives to come by first thing tomorrow? To set up the phone trap?"

"Sure. Let's just hope there are no calls tonight."

He looked at me, perhaps considering a defense of policework, where speed is not always possible. "Yes," was all he said. He looked tired and hot.

"You just come from a workout?"

"Sort of." He eyed the lawn chairs.

I took the cue. "Not a foot chase, I hope. Let's sit by the pool." I mentioned my visit with A.J.

"Yes," Compoz affirmed. "Dugan questioned him last Sunday. Wrote him up as helpful, but with no information

79

that led anywhere." He went on to say he'd followed up Dugan's first interviews with the homeowners on the cul de sac. "Especially Mrs. Rauch at fifteen-forty. She was home at the time of the incident."

Mrs. Rauch with no sympathy for backyard trespassers.

"She had nothing new to tell me. I noticed a kid shooting hoops at the back of the house. Right where the fence edges the cul de sac." Compoz took several deep breaths. "Been a long time since I played basketball. I used to be on the police team."

A vague sadness in his voice kept me from asking why he had no time for sports now.

"I decided to go a little one-on-one with the kid. Get rapport, you know. I held my own for the first few minutes. Then . . ." He grinned.

I liked this warmer Compoz, no longer cool as his cool green shirt.

"When we took a breather, I asked if he knew about the hit-and-run. He said yes, but he'd left just about dusk that day to go to a buddy's house. So I figured I'd ruined the starch in my shirt for nothing." He ran his thumbs down the back of his tie. "Still, I asked if he'd seen anything unusual."

The sergeant smiled, unafraid to make eye contact. Not all cops do. "The kid tells me, 'Listen, I see something unusual *every* day.' " Compoz shook his head. "Then he let me eat dust on four layups before he said, 'Matter of fact, I did see something that afternoon. An old junker car. I figured one of the gays was in there parking, and it died on him.' "

The Sergeant leaned forward, intent, his eyes on the pool like he might dive right in. "I asked the kid what did it look like, what color was it? 'From the dark ages, man

— Frankie and Annette time. Throw-up green. With gigantic fins.' " Compoz turned to me. "Bingo. Our first break."

"The color sure jibes. Frankie and Annette — that's the sixties. Dugan was right about it being an old car with a big engine."

"Right place and right time too," Compoz said, his eyes back on the water. Then he added with a smile, "I always liked Annette."

9

BEACH BUNNY REVOLT

The hordes descended bright and early. First Detective
Franz — he might have slept in his suit. Then the phone
company installer, with her tool belt slung at a jaunty
angle. She offered an intimate smile. Up the drive came
Sandal and Gladdie, singing "Let the Sunshine In," and
carrying a bag of hot croissants. "Take the day off," they
called. "We want to go play."

In his short robe, Marty hardly looked an appropriate
waiter, but he poured everyone coffee while Gladdie

divided the croissants. The cop ate his roll in two bites. "All set," the installer said, and held out her clipboard for Franz to sign. While he wasn't looking, she winked at Gladdie.

"Sergeant Compoz wanted me to give you this," Franz said, handing me a large envelope and shifting the wadded shoulders of his coat. Then he and the installer left our kaffee klatsch.

Compoz had sent me the skid photo and a note. "Call me before you use this. I've got some more on the brick. Dugan's coming by about ten if you want to join us — my office."

Audrey Louise came in, and I told everyone about the break we'd had on the car. Sandal described our visit with A.J. and Robin. "I remember Gaither," Marty said. "Fair-haired boy, isn't he? But no great brain. I had the vague impression he didn't write his own papers. No proof —just a feeling."

Everyone agreed we needed a play day. Marty was persuaded to cancel his office hours. We planned to drop by Category Six, then head to Patience and Sarah's for champagne brunch. I would reconnect with them after my meeting.

At the Denver police building, Compoz and Dugan were feeling hopeful. "Roy's got a make on the car," the Sergeant said.

Commander Dugan liked the story he had to tell me. "My buddy Covelli, big Italian fella, runs a garage in LaJunta. Keeps a card file where he's logged paint samples from every car he's worked on in thirty years. He put our green rust under a damned microscope." Dugan whistled with pleasure, and grinned at me. "Covelli matched it with a sixty-six Bel Air. That was the last year of Chevy's big fins before they trimmed back."

83

Compoz nodded. "Which links up with the Rauch boy's description."

"It's not a lab test, but my money's on the Italian. And we did a backup with the FBI, just in case some whiz kid goes to work for them and makes a dent in their backload. Meantime, I'm running a list out of DMV," Dugan added.

"How many do you figure you'll have?" I asked.

"Let's just hope it's not two thousand," Dugan said, rolling one big shoulder. Then he asked Compoz, "Your guys scare up anything at the college?"

"Not a hint. The regents assure us there's no campus group with any resemblance to the Foresters, nor has such a group ever existed. Dr. Evans and Professor Stevens are held in the highest regard by students and colleagues alike."

"Tell us something we don't know," I said. "How come I get to use the skid photo, Sergeant?"

He straightened his tie — this one a wild blue paisley. "I can't prove these events are connected, but my gut tells me they are. My gut also tells me the sequence is backwards. First the hit-and-run, then this petty stuff. That really bothers me. I figure we've got two choices. Keep our cards close to our vest, or lay them on the table. Say we think there's a link, name the group, announce we've I.D.'d the car. They'll either stop dead in their tracks, or ..."

"Or commit another violent crime."

His eyes told me of a wish to reassure that he couldn't give. "Maybe we can flush them. Or force a mistake that lets us nail them."

I didn't like the sound of it, but I was willing to do my part. Even as I began to feel that my garage apartment sanctuary was suddenly vulnerable.

Dugan picked up the brick on Compoz's desk and examined it. Two small holes had been drilled for sample extraction. "My lab tech says this is soft-mud brick," Compoz told us, "based on water content in the clay. It's Colorado shale, year dated to nineteen-oh-six. With some traces of soot, as if the brick'd been in a fire, although the tech says fire bricks per se are an entirely different size and composition. He took it to the brick museum in Pueblo, they told him it was made by hand, using something called a repress machine. They think it might be a special commemorative brick."

"Those lab boys are something," Dugan exulted. The two cops grinned at each other.

"Now we just track down the Denver building history for that year, pinpoint what's still standing and what's been torn down, where the scrap bricks went, where they are today." Compoz smiled. "Routine police work. And they say this job is no fun."

When I walked into the bookstore, I crashed a birthday party. Six wimmin were clustered around a cake, about to blow out the candles. I recognized the two sisters I'd seen before, but all of the wimmin wore turquoise bandannas — exactly the color of the lotus on Pat's notebook; I wondered if they were displaying colors. My eyes met those of the younger denim-clad sister. She stared back, holding me with her smoldering eyes. Was that anger, or a challenge?

"P.D. is turning the big three-oh," Neal called to me. "Have some cake."

"Please don't start with let them eat cake," Dan teased his lover.

My own entourage of Audrey Louise and Marty had joined in the celebration, but were now engrossed in the bookshelves. Marty soon brought me a plate. "Audrey Louise has bought eighty dollars worth of books," he said, grinning. At which point she came around the corner with her own broad smile. "You ready for champagne?" she asked.

"I'm ready to write one helluva story. We got a make on the car."

"What is it?" Marty squeezed my hand.

"A sixty-six Bel Air."

"Sounds almost too friendly," Audrey Louise said. Then she asked Neal confidentially, "Are those wimmin with the bandannas a gang or something?"

"More like a guild," he answered. "Guild of the Benevolent Protectoress."

At that moment a most unlikely pair came into the store. Gene Nile from the GLCC, and Crazy Mary. She darted among the other people, and snatched a piece of cake in one disco glove.

"Nyla, I'm glad to see you," Gene called to me. "You'll want to hear my news."

I wasn't the only one — everyone in the store stopped to listen. "The Foresters paid a visit to the Center this morning. Glue in the door locks and some of their flyers, just like here. But that's a minor irritation. The phone's been ringing off the hook. Seems the parks patrol isn't just interviewing about the hit-and-run. They're muscling up the gay people at Cheesman."

"He's right, I seen 'em." The voice sounded like cold beads in a tin box. Crazy Mary. "Roustin' the fairies for no good reason. Playin' booby snatch on the girls."

"You're kidding," I said, stepping up close enough to see raindrop stains on the letters of her Mets cap. "You saw patrolmen touch those wimmin?"

"I seen 'em."

I wanted to see for myself. We must have seemed an odd crew: one disillusioned justice-chaser followed by an Aurora Earth Mother, professor emeritus, and the poncho and muu-muu duet. At a safe distance, the guild also headed for Cheesman. And somewhere among the trees was Crazy Mary.

The standoff had begun. About a hundred people had staked their territory between the pools and the columns. Mostly men in shorts and swim suits, more playful than menacing as they splashed each other and snapped their towels. A few wimmin looked more serious. Beer cans flashed in the sunlight.

Three police vehicles were parked up on the grass by the fountains. But luckily there was no SWAT team in sight. A shouting match was going on between two patrolmen and a smaller group — three men and a womon. "You got no right," one of the men yelled. "You're just screwin' us over. Everyone's told you what we know."

"Get your damned armor out of here, this is our turf," one of the other men screamed.

"This is nobody's turf. This is a Denver city park. You're here as a privilege. The rules are for everyone."

"Yeah, you're not hassling everyone," the womon yelled.

The other patrolmen stood by, as if waiting for reinforcements. I didn't recognize any rank on their uniforms, so I approached two of them standing by a cruiser. Flashing my CNB press card, I asked, "What's the trouble here?"

They didn't answer. Then one asked to see the card again. He gave it a long look. Scanned the crowd, and said, "Something about us bruising their gay rights. I didn't think gays had any rights."

Sandal talked to several wimmin, then reported to me. "They say there was some touchy-feely going on, just one cop. He claims a dyke swung at him and he had to defend himself."

"I better call Compoz. Then see if CNB wants to get pictures." I turned to look back toward the shout-athon. Caught the flash of turquoise as a tall womon stepped in between the officers and the protesters. Something happened within the crowd, a quieting. And indeed the peace maker had arrived. Within a few minutes, the patrolmen got into their cars. One car drove to the far perimeter, but the rest of the vehicles left the park. The beach bunnies slowly dispersed, back to their towels and private conversations.

"Who are those wimmin?" I asked.

Gene Nile appeared at my elbow and answered, "The Parker sisters. Tell is the older one, Scout looks enough like her to be a twin."

The twin appeared, as did the four other sisters of the turquoise scarves, who moved easily among the crowd — calling to friends, laughing, taking the charge out of the air.

"Maybe they ought to be called the Power sisters," I said.

* * * * *

At the CNB office, Bead swooped in on me and snapped out questions like an agitated terrier. "Taking your sweet time filing a story," she chattered before I even had my first sheet of paper in the typewriter. I fended her off with the skid photo and the Forester flyer. Told her quickly about the near-miss Lavender Revolt in Cheesman.

"This really *is* Homophobia Beserka," she said. Then zipped out the door. "I'm calling the News. This is right up their alley."

As I wrote the story, I could feel a quickening in myself. Like all the engines were stoked again. Like hope had returned. Maybe it was the crowd, or the instant camaraderie at the bookstore. Whatever it was, I used it for fuel. Even when Bead came in and read over my shoulder. "You've got it, Wade," she breathed. "By gawd, you've got it."

My story called for a citizens' alert on the Bel Air. Praised the men in blue, and told the tale of brick-bombs and brick marks. Showed the paradox of violent conservatism. Now we would wait and see if it brought the Foresters out of the trees.

10
THE SHALLOWS

After I left the CNB office, two questions nagged me. What would the Foresters next move be, and what would Rose Stevens think when she read my article? I felt more ready to deal with the Sons of God than one mother who would have to confront her daughter's lesbianism under such difficult circumstances.

Back at the apartment, I sat on the deck rereading Pat's poems.

When I'm afraid, you fight for me
Without armor, with only a cloak of hope
And the sword of love.

I imagined her finding the Foresters' pink notes in her mailbox, or dropped just inside her screen door. I wondered how she kept the paranoia monsters at bay, how she convinced herself the harassment would end. Who had she believed would fight for her now that Lou had gone? I felt the leather spine of the notebook like a backbone proving itself. Like Pat's own voice convincing me I had the courage to take up the sword of love.

When I called Sergeant Compoz to discuss the Parks Patrol, he already knew about it.

"All they do is roust vagrants and enforce curfew. They probably got bored. I've called their commander."

"Isn't it a dead issue by now — finding a witness, I mean? It's been nearly a week."

He sighed audibly. "Yes, it probably is. But we have to try everything. Certainly this business in the park doesn't help."

When I asked if he'd narrowed down the DMV list, he sighed again. "Would you believe a hundred and eight sixty-six Bel Airs in Denver? Dugan's got a bunch of his guys helping. We're ringing the phones off the hook."

The call disheartened me — too many cars to track down, what if the crime car was registered out of state, or not registered at all? What if the green paint had been popular in sixty-six on more than Bel Airs? Maybe we were just wasting our time.

* * * * *

Thursday evening — four days since Pat had been run down — finished in suburban quietude far from political confrontations and metro crime. Joel barbecued while Marty swam with the boys, who argued about which one could grow his hair the fastest, to get a "tail" cut like Marty's. Audrey Louise told me I looked tired. "Your story go okay?"

"You can read all about it in the *News*."

I decided to take on the tribe in the pool. "Your suit's in the washer," Audrey Louise told me. "Just change in the boys' room."

Amid a nightmare jumble of tennis shoes, food wrappers, and He-Man dolls, I stripped down. I had the pink Speedo stretched just up to my waist when Audrey Louise's oldest boy Sam walked in on me.

"So you're a lesbian," he said, his unabashed eyes on my bare breasts. "Is it more fun?"

"Than what?"

"You know, than with guys."

"I happen to think so." I forced the suit straps over my shoulders.

He scratched an ear. "Well, you could be in trouble. Colorado has the ERA, but boys can't be lesbians."

My article lit up the switchboard at the *Rocky Mountain News* — so Bead reported early on Friday. "Someone from Colorado Antique Cars Association thinks we've put an onus on Bel Airs. A woman in Arvada swears that space aliens left a pink flyer in her mailbox. Five calls came in from people who want to join the Foresters. But we got ten times as many calls from people outraged by the group's violence. One live one — a mason told me marks are common on bricks made by hand.

Everything from owls and sunflowers to a mason's initials. Sometimes words misspelled or letters reversed on purpose. That's a mason's sense of humor."

"Needle in a haystack," I said, thinking about all the bricks made in 1906, and 108 Bel Airs.

Seemed Compoz had read the story with his first cup of coffee, then called me. "You stung 'em good," he said. "And the timing might work. It's party night, maybe they'll target some of the gay bars. Just in case, patrol will be making extra passes. You and Dr. Evans might want to stay close to home." He said he'd contacted the Parks Patrol commander. "But it's party night in the park too. I hope there's no more trouble."

Another call came in from Gene Nile. "You tell it like it is, Nyla. But aren't the cops worried this will incite the Foresters to more violence?"

I relayed Compoz's concerns. "I had the same thought," Nile said. "I'm going to call some of the bar owners."

I asked Marty if he had time to drop me at the hospital on his way to D.C.C. He'd planned to go anyway. On the drive, we talked about the story. "Compoz thinks it might tip their hand," I said.

"Yeah, using me to place his bet."

His sarcasm put me on the defensive. "I know he doesn't see it that way. DPD has followed up every shred of evidence there is. There's nowhere else to go. Maybe I'm the one who's put you in jeopardy — I wrote the story."

"Sorry," he muttered. "I'm just frustrated."

And scared, I could tell by looking at him. Because I was scared too.

At least Rose wasn't reading the *Rocky Mountain News* when we found her in the waiting room. But she'd seen it — I could tell by the expectancy in her face, and the way she held my eyes.

"Anything new with Pat?" Marty asked. She shook her head. "You see the article?"

"Yes."

I didn't know what to say. Part of me wanted to apologize for dredging around in her family dynamic. Another part of me wanted to tell her that if ever Pat needed her support, it was now.

"This is hard for me to understand." She stood up and moved to the window. "Why someone could hurt Pat on purpose." She turned back to face us. "And you too, Marty."

I felt too uncomfortable to sit. "Mrs. Stevens, the facts had to come out. But I didn't mean to add to your pain."

She studied me, her face revealing nothing of her thoughts. She patted a stray lock of silver-grey hair at the nape of her neck. "I used to look at Pat and wonder, Who is that person that looks so much like my daughter, yet is another being entirely outside my understanding? I couldn't talk about it, not even to my husband.

"You just never expect to find out one of your children is homosexual. There was my daughter, somehow with a change in identity, like a double image of the same face that blurs all the familiar lines. Then, after Stephen . . ."

She turned to stare out the window. "When he disappeared, I washed the floors and walls of his room until the paint discolored. Washed his sheets and towels over and over again. I remember folding them so deliberately . . ." She took a deep breath, felt her neck for the loose hair again. "I folded away most of my feelings then too, especially for Pat."

She turned back to us, with a return of strength in her eyes — and sadness. For the lost opportunities, and the misunderstanding. For the isolation. "When I look at her now, she's Pat again. And regardless of whether I ever agree with her choices, she doesn't deserve to pay for them with her life."

I was surprised when Marty went to her, put his arm around her shoulders. "It may not be over," he said.

Rose nodded, fighting tears. "At least this time she's not alone. Neither of us is."

Marty let me off in Cheesman Park at Franklin Street. "I want to be sure no one's stirring up the sunbathers," I told him.

"See you later, sleuth."

"Come right home, okay?"

"Are we having dinner in protective custody?" At least he was smiling. I watched him drive off, and fought the uneasy feeling in my stomach.

How different it felt walking in the park now than last Sunday. I wondered if Crazy Mary skulked through the trees nearby. Did she know the Gauntlet? Maybe that's where courage and swords could be found.

Sun bounced too bright off the pools, and I shielded my eyes. Looked up toward the cool shade of the bandshell and heard music. The twang of Bob Dylan singing, "If you want somebody to trust, trust yourself." I recognized the wimmin clustered around the boom box by their turquoise bandannas.

Tell Parker moved toward me at once, her hand extended, and introducing herself. "Read your story this morning. This is my sister Scout. And our friends: Gracie, Slim, P.D., and Coral."

At last a formal introduction. I had a chance to look at all of them in turn. Gracie with a face full of tough life, but she had pretty ears and soft grey hair. She wore her bandanna around her boot top. Slim stood as tall as the Parkers; her straight blonde hair was parted in the center. Dressed in full leathers, she'd tied on her bandanna as a headband. Coral danced nervously to Dylan, grinning and humming, shaking a belt of turquoise scarf around her hips. P.D. raised one leather-gloved fist as greeting. Short, dark, and solidly muscled, she'd wrapped the bandanna around her wrist above the glove.

"P.D.," Coral giggled. "For Pretty Damned Dykey."

"So you're working with the Denver police on all this," Scout said. Her scarf hung through a loop of her jeans like a limp boomerang.

"Yes, I am."

"Is it legit?" Tell asked. "I mean, having the Parks Patrol get in everyone's business."

"They were supposed to be searching for witnesses."

"Which means DPD has zip," Scout glowered.

"They have a puzzle. With a lot of missing pieces."

"Yeah," P.D. snickered. "Like their brains." Coral laughed, a sound too loose at the edges.

"They doing anything to protect Marty Evans?" Tell asked. "We know him."

I understood her implication. "They've beefed up the patrol, and our calls are being traced."

"Right," Scout scoffed. "I bet he feels real safe."

I wanted to tell her her mouth was too supple for so much snarling. I saved my breath on a speech about policework and the toll it takes to put your face into murder and rape every single day and still care about the unprovable hit-and-run of one lesbian.

"We know Denver cops," P.D. said. "They forget to arrange lineups. Forget to follow up with lawyers. They lose evidence. Mostly they just lose interest."

"Fast," Scout said. "Very fast." She twirled her scarf, then flicked it like a soft lariat into a loop around Tell's wrist.

"They don't see us as people," Tell added. "A lot of us live down on Broadway Terrace. The cops call it the gay ghetto. You call in for help, they take their time getting there."

I wasn't about to argue for either side. Didn't have Tell's peace maker knack for stepping in between stereotypes — lesbians dubbing cops as flatfoot dummies, cops labeling gay wimmin as man-hating diesel dykes. "Maybe we're wasting time pointing fingers. I know about cops too. No sense trying to pretend things are fair. But in this case, they're trying everything."

Tell ran her bandanna back and forth across her neck. I could see the design of a black thunderbolt against the bluegreen scarf. I liked the moment of softness in her eyes. I said, "My contact in Assault has talked with the Parks Patrol commander. With any luck, they'll let up."

Tell held my eyes, and I could feel the strong presence of each of her companions. "Okay," she said. "We'll pass the word."

At that moment the bandshell echoed with a shriek. Down on the grass by the pools, Crazy Mary had been nabbed by the Parks Patrol.

Two officers had her, holding her arms as she struggled to break free. Like a broken rainbow, the Sisters of the Scarves ran through the trees. I ran toward the policemen.

"What do you know about that hit-and-run, old lady?" One patrolman shook Mary by her arm. "We know you camp out in that cul de sac. Now tell us what you saw!"

She dug in her heels and dragged both men backward.

As I reached them, P.D. and Gracie came in from behind, hitting the officers at the knees. All four of them went down, and Crazy Mary plunged straight into the reflecting pool. She surged through the water until the weight of her layered clothing slowed her down. One officer wrenched away from Gracie and hit the water. I went in after both of them.

"She's scared, for chrissakes, stop chasing her!" I yelled at him. "We know her, we'll get her to talk." The water was icy cold despite the spring sun.

He dove at Crazy Mary but she skittered just out of his reach. He dove again and snatched her dress. She peeled out of it and strained forward. Cursing and splashing, the two of them clambered toward the other side of the pool.

"Stop chasing her!" I yelled again.

Mary made it out of the pool first, but she was only three steps ahead of the furious patrolman. Just as he reached to grab her, I saw a coil of turquoise snag his ankles, and down he went. I landed right on top of him. Crazy Mary dashed into the trees.

The conversation between Compoz and the Parks Patrol commander was a noisy one. They squared off next to the sergeant's Caprice. The commander pounded on the car several times. The sergeant raised his voice. Our joust with the patrolmen had apparently ruffled jurisdictional feathers. Eventually they agreed not to charge us with anything. Certainly Compoz and DPD had greater authority, but he'd probably conceded a favor anyway just to placate the Parks Patrol commander.

I doubted the Parker sisters and their guild would give him any credit, though, and hoped they wouldn't ignite a surly confrontation. He left the commander and approached us. "You're all free to go," he said.

Even the guild seemed surprised. "No charges?" Tell asked.

"I told him I'd warn you. You're warned."

"You gonna call out the troops after Mary?" Scout asked in a hard-edged voice.

Compoz met her eyes. "Could she know something? She is a regular in the park. This isn't the first time the patrol has picked her up."

"People gotta have a place to sleep," P.D. defended her.

"I'm asking you if she might have information to help us find whoever ran over Pat Stevens in this park last Sunday. Not whether the woman has a right to sleep here."

Scout tensed; Tell put a hand on her arm. "We'll see if we can find her. Try to talk to her. If she does know anything..."

Compoz gave her one of his cards. "Call me. We need a lead." He knew his priorities. False pride wasn't one of them.

We sat in the Caprice as the sisters departed and the commander mustered his frustrated warriors. I didn't

100

know if Compoz wanted me to apologize, but I didn't intend to.

"You heard any reaction about the article?" he asked.

"Yeah. Masons have a sense of humor."

Neither Compoz nor I really believed the Foresters would be so bold as to drive their '66 Bel Air close enough to a Denver gay bar to toss another brick-bomb. And yet, I think both of us hoped lightning would strike somewhere — that the car, fat as a tank and hospital-green, would flash its fins in the wrong place and the right person would see it. But I couldn't just sit in Aurora waiting for the phone to ring, or worrying about Marty. I walked from Cheesman over to the GLCC.

Gene Nile didn't balk when I asked him to spend the evening driving around with me to Denver's gay bars. "You onto some urgent clue?" he asked. All I answered was, "Just a hunch. Just restless." And when I asked him to stop at a 7-11 so I could call a psychic friend, he warmed up to the adventure even more.

Gladdie seemed happy to hear from me — asked about Pat and Marty and the police. I told her about Crazy Mary. Knew if she was trying to read my mind, she'd find it full of swords and layers of wet dresses and lightning and cars finned like dragons. "I've just got this hunch about tonight and I wanted to call you. See if you heard any odd rhymes in your head today." I laughed.

"Don't be embarassed, Nyla. I appreciate your asking. Your trusting my gift." She paused a moment; I could hear a loud whooshing in the background.

"Sandal's using the sandblaster," she told me. So she could read some thoughts. Then she added, "No rhymes today. Just one word. I have no idea how it will help you. *Palomino.*"

We started our peculiar patrol at Mister Michael's. Mostly Mercedes were parked in that lot. The place didn't have the look of a gay bar — no front windows blanked out with black paint, no dark street front between warehouses.

"Not much trouble here, I bet."

"You'd be surprised. Michael has replaced the front windows five times."

At the Triangle Lounge, only a block from the Federal Building and chambers of city justice, motorcycle chrome flashed like muscled mirrors. Men in studded outfits dismounted their noisy machines, flexing their chaps, stiff caps, sweaty leather gloves. I stared. Gene laughed.

"Who in their right mind would try to pick a fight here?" I asked, as another cycle roared in, revved by a barechested man wearing a black leather vest. His biker buddy hung onto him by clasping two handfuls of copious chest hair.

"On enough beer, there's no such thing as a fierce fairy," Gene said.

The oldest Denver wimmin's bar, Three Sisters, hugged the highway in the barrio. One pale light shone over the adobe door. Across the street, Spanish music blared from the El Cordobes bar. Several men hung out in the doorway and passed a bottle. "Clash of cultures?" I asked Gene.

"Sometimes. But they give each other a wide berth."

We pulled into the parking lot — I wished it weren't so

dark. Wished we were enjoying the spring night air instead of cruising for that shark of a car.

A brawny security cop directed cars into the lot at Divine Madness. "The new lesbian bar," Gene said. "They're doing it right. Their own security. No drugs or under age kids. No payola either."

He pulled up next to the cop. "How's it going tonight?"

The man smiled. "Hey there, Gene. Thanks for the call. We're busy tonight, but no trouble."

We headed back to Capitol Hill. "Unless the Foresters are kamikazes," Gene said, "they'd never buzz Cheesman tonight. But I wonder, maybe we ought to check the Shallows."

We drove toward the state capitol building, with its dome glowing in the dark as if it held a dollop of sun in its night gold. I asked, "Has the action in the park slowed at all because of AIDS? That's more dangerous than being out in the open for bushwackers and the police."

"True," he told me. "But there are still too many men willing to take that life-or-death risk for the sex prowl. The element of danger is part of the excitement."

I just shook my head. We parked on Grant Street, the outside perimeter of the Capitol parking lot. A small lot, really, that circled the building — we could see the East steps.

"That's called the Grand Back Door," Gene said. "In more ways than one."

As my eyes grew used to the dark, I could see a continuous row of car lights circling the lot and stopping near the steps. When a car stopped, someone would come out from behind the steps. "Hustlers?" I asked.

"Chickens," Gene answered. "Most of them runaways. Most of them gay."

103

"And the buyers?"

"Married men from the suburbs."

"Aren't they scared of AIDS?"

"Not scared enough. They drive in here every night like fish to spawn. It's a cheap thrill. Twenty bucks for a fast trick."

We sat and watched the crawl of cars — headlights, brake lights, inside light as a kid got in. "They usually drive a block or two over, do their business, and then the kid walks back here to wait for the next trick." We watched, and the million glimmering eyes of the stars watched this bizarre ritual — not love or mating or even sex. Something else, I decided, a search for a touch, however elusive and brutal, to the core of forbidden feelings. A moment of reality that had to do with the untold soul.

"Anyone can drive in here and buy." Gene sighed. "No one's gonna memorize a face. What if the Foresters came here. Got hold of one of these kids." He shook his head. "I don't call it the Shallows. I call it the Sorrows."

The cars kept circling, searching souls with everything to fear, yet nothing stopped them. As nothing seemed to stop the Foresters. Because we could not find the common link, could not say which familiar face knew enough to put Pat and Marty in jeopardy.

Over by a water fountain, a blond boy who'd come from the steps walked into the light of a street lamp. He ran his hands full of water and splashed it over his face and hair, then tipped his head back as if asking the moon for a blow dry. I couldn't see his face, or what his eyes would tell of this life in the Shallows. He seemed like a misplaced beauty, only on the periphery of these sorrows.

As I watched him, I thought about our search beginning and ending on the periphery of two lives,

104

causing us to doubt Pat and Marty's friends, and the more uncertain farther-reaching chain of their friends — a whole lineup of faces unknown to us. The blond boy reminded me of someone else. Someone we thought had told us all he knew and seemed to have no secrets. Yet through him, I realized someone else could have moved from the periphery to the heart of Pat and Marty's lives.

11
DOMINOS

Gene couldn't get me back to Aurora fast enough. When I stepped into the living room, Tony had just toppled the first domino in an outline of the United States. On hands and knees, he and Marty laughed as the other dominos fell. "There goes Iowa!"

"Look out Nebraska!"

Audrey Louise brought a platter of fudge wedges from the kitchen. She watched her son, saying, "Tony and his adult pals. Sandal and Gladdie want to take him to an antique show tomorrow. Should I worry?"

"Only if he asks for a poncho."

When the states had fallen, Tony wanted to set up an outline of the world.

Marty declined, asking me, "Did you stir up any clues?"

"Yeah, especially on that brick," Tony chimed in. "That was a neato part of your story."

"Nothing more on the brick, I'm afraid. Just the year it was made and those traces of soot." To the others I said, "We need to talk."

We left Tony scanning an atlas, and went out onto the back porch. "Since we're getting nowhere fast," I started in, "let me try out some ideas on you. We've assumed the notes and phone calls Pat received when she lived with Lou had nothing to do with the recent set of notes. We also assume, based on the pink paper and the phrasing, that this second set came from the Foresters. Let's merge assumptions. Say all the notes came from the Foresters."

"From what she told you, though," Marty argued, "she thought the first notes were just a prank by students. This latest set seems connected to the Foresters' attack on the whole gay community."

"Suppose it only seemed that way to her. The first notes and calls occurred at the same time the Foresters made their first appearance, vandalizing that doctor's house and harassing the nurse and teacher."

"Okay," Audrey Louise played along. "So they're part of a bigger plot. How does that help? Sounds to me like it distances a common denominator even more."

"Not if someone known to Pat and Marty is also known to the Foresters. It's been impossible to peg any

107

friend for the connection. So let's look in another direction. Someone who's a pipeline of information without knowing it. In other words, an unwitting stoolie."

"Don't talk like Bogart." Marty sounded frustrated.

"You mean our common denominator is once-removed from motive?" Audrey Louise said.

"Exactly. We've been wracking our brains about Pat and Marty's friends and co-workers who could have such a skewed motive. If we ignore motive temporarily, maybe we can find the pipeline."

"Sounds like so much guesswork to me," Marty grumbled.

"What's the plan?" Audrey Louise stayed on the point.

"We concentrate on timing. Verify if the first notes and calls did occur during the same time frame as the early Forester harassment. Then determine when the new notes started, and look at that time frame. Most important, we figure out who was in Pat's life during both those periods, who knew about her general schedule and the changes going on. Not all the details, but enough. Someone who could also know Marty."

"Those are guesses the size of Texas," he groaned. "The only person who knows the exact timing of all this is Pat."

His remark silenced us for a moment, reminded us too clearly of her absence.

Audrey Louise tried to be encouraging. "She could come out of the coma any time."

"Or never," Marty snapped. "Hell, there are no prints or witnesses to link the Foresters to any of this. And by now that car is long gone — painted, repaired, or dumped in a canyon."

"Guesswork and luck — Commander Dugan swears by both. We're guessing all right, but we're luckier than you think, Marty. For one thing, someone else knows the timing of the first notes."

"Who?"

"Lou Diablo."

"Now wait just a minute. If you think I'm gonna follow up that lead, think again. I told you, we didn't part on the best of terms."

"And for another thing," I continued, "I already know who our common denominator is."

They both stared at me. "Remember, disregard motive and focus on that open channel of information. Someone who knew you both at the college. Knew Pat at her apartment. Even knew her running schedule. Knew the complete layout of the cul de sac, in fact. And in causal conversation, could have relayed important details about you both to someone else."

Marty's eyes shone with hot energy. "A.J."

I nodded.

Audrey Louise flipped on the lights around the pool and stared out at them. "Didn't he tell you that he'd never heard the rumors about Pat and Lou?"

"Yes. Which would make him all the more unsuspecting with someone who *had.* Someone who saw Pat and Lou as new victims."

"I don't think Pat considered A.J. a peer," Marty protested. "And I certainly don't think she shared any confidences with him."

"She didn't have to, Marty. A.J. could still reveal exactly what Pat's assailant needed to know — when she ran, and where. But even more important, that she'd be running alone that Sunday night."

Audrey Louise turned back to us. "But how could A.J. have known about Marty coming here for dinner, the night he was brick-bashed?"

We'd reached assumptions breakdown — I didn't have a good guess for that question. Until I looked at Marty's face. He'd gone completely white. "A.J. called the hospital that night to ask about Pat. Offered to bring me dinner. I told him I was coming out here."

"And he knew my name from our talk with Commander Dugan," Audrey Louise remembered. "Easy enough to get the address from the phone book."

The pool lights made wavy shadows on the new fence. "Marty, do you know when A.J. was Pat's student?"

"No, but I can find out from the registrar's office. Which will be a helluva lot easier than finding out when the new notes were sent."

I looked directly at him "But we can find out about the first notes." I wondered if Lou would even talk to him, much less remember a Forester flyer.

My former guru of the Passionate Few was looking now like the Intimidated One. For a moment I thought he might tell me to go to hell, or stomp out into the night. I told him what Pat had shared with me on our walk in the park, her realizations that she had been suffocating Lou. When I finished, he sat for some minutes watching the water and the lights, as if the pool had become some ghost-dancing acrylic sculpture. Finally he said, "Sandal can give us Lou's number in Egypt."

At midnight in Denver, Marty reached Lou starting her morning in Cairo. "She was surprised," he told us, "but her old self. When I asked 'How's the desert?' she answered, 'Dusty.' " His news about Pat shocked her, and she was most willing to help. She recalled receiving two notes — the pink paper and the pine tree sounded familiar, but the Foresters didn't ring a bell. She was sure of the misspelling, though: Q-W-E-A-R. "We laughed it off, you can't take those things seriously. Knowing Pat, she probably dated it and put it in a file."

That possibility sounded like a stroke of luck to us, and we agreed to search Pat's apartment. Marty said he felt lucky in another way. "An apology, even one that comes late, can begin a healing."

Around ten o'clock on Saturday, an insistent tapping at the apartment door wakened me from my dream. A dream born in wetness and sweet heat. Lovers' sighs and locked thighs, moans and promises kept. Dents from bellies and breasts left in summer-night sand. I could feel Lucy to the ends of my hair as I grabbed a robe.

Gladdie wore stone-washed jeans and a yellow sweatshirt — she looked strong and hopeful standing there on my doorstep. Held up two cups of coffee and asked, "Did your hunch pay off last night?"

We sat on the deck, and I described the Shallows and the blond boy in the moonlight who had reminded me of A.J. Farrell. Then our guesswork and the luck we hoped to find in Pat's apartment. "Ah," Gladdie sighed. "I see why I thought of palominos. Not meaning a golden horse, but golden boys instead." She mused, gazing at the tulips and pansies in the yard below. "I had also thought it might mean a horse of a different color."

Tony danced in in his bermuda shorts and perfectly polished Bass loafers. He held out his hand for her. "Good luck with your search," she said.

I went with them down to the driveway. Marty said he was off to the registrar's office. A vague image at the back of my mind made me ask him to get the entire class roster.

Audrey Louise shooed the other boys into the station wagon. "They feel cheated, so I'm taking them to a matinee. *Godzilla versus Mothra.*" She grimaced, then hailed Marty. "What time should we go to Pat's apartment?"

He shook his head. "I don't relish the idea of rifling through Pat's belongings. I'd feel better somehow if Rose came along with us. And I think she would welcome a chance to help."

"Give her something to do besides waiting," I said. "I could pick her up now, and you two could meet us there."

"Good idea." Marty tossed me the keys to Pat's apartment. "She's got a storage locker in the basement."

"You can take Joel's car," Audrey Louise offered as Marty drove away. She looked at her two sons wrestling in the back seat. "I didn't sleep much last night, thinking about those young boys in the Shallows." She brushed one hand across her hair. "Such sadness . . . I feel for them."

I was in the shower when the phone rang. For a panicky moment I wondered if the Foresters had my number. Hoped the phone trap was fool proof. I was relieved to hear Compoz's voice.

"All quiet out there in Aurora?"

"Nothing shaking but the sprinkler systems."

"Good. Maybe your article chased the Foresters back underground. In the meantime, I just pulled up a doozy on the NIP."

"The what?"

He laughed. "Our Nippon computer, state crime-stats database. I was scanning those Bel Air owners for any criminal record. And I found just the gold nugget we need."

The excitement in his voice made my heart pound. If we found the car, we'd be one step from finding the Foresters. And Pat's attacker.

"One of the owners is a guy named Levere Eller. Former employee of Denver Community College. Also a former student. But less than a gentleman, it seems. The college filed assault charges against him. Surprise, surprise — based on a complaint from Pat Stevens."

"Sounds like just the lead we've been looking for," I exclaimed.

"That's not all. I checked with D.C.C. Seems the run-in also involved Professor Evans."

"When were those charges filed, Sergeant?"

"Hold on a sec." I could hear him rustling papers. "Here it is. May fifth, nineteen-eighty six."

Just a few weeks before the Foresters advertised in red paint, I thought. Why hadn't Marty mentioned this?

Compoz reminded me that Marty and I weren't yet out of danger. "This deal on the car may not pan out, and the Foresters may just be biding their time."

Before I went to the hospital, I phoned Bead to clue her in on the latest. "K,L, K,L — the letters on that damned brick are keeping me up nights," she whined. "I even went to the brick museum myself. Learned to dissect frogs." She laughed, a sound like a warped finger-harp.

"Frog," she said, "the indentation in a green clay brick that contains a decorative marking. Also makes the brick burn well. They told me two things at the museum

— there's no record of any commemorative bricks in the whole state for nineteen-oh-six. Yet the letters on our frog weren't drawn free-hand, like someone's initials." She sounded stymied, but determined. "When you know more about the car, give me an update. Especially if they take Eller in for questioning."

At first glance, Rose Stevens seemed to be turning as grey as the grey-blue linen suit she wore. A magazine lay open in her lap, and she stared at the sun bouncing off the lower roof of the hospital's west wing. But somehow its warmth eluded her.

She was glad to see me, asked immediately about the police investigation. Compoz's news about the Bel Air encouraged her, along with what we'd turned up from talking with Lou. "If we can find that flyer, and it has a date on it, maybe we can put the pieces together."

She glanced toward the door to Pat's room, then took a deep breath. "All right, Nyla. Let's start the search."

As I unlocked the door to Pat's apartment, Rose waited expectantly. The rooms were too warm, so she immediately opened the kitchen window. Stood there a moment, taking in every nuance of Pat's space. Could she know how hard it had been to claim it without Lou? "The flyer we're looking for will be on pink paper, easy to spot." I showed her my copy of the Forester manifesto — reading it obviously pained her. "You want to start with Pat's desk? I'll do the file cabinet."

It seemed natural to take her arm as we went to the bedroom. Just inside the door, Rose stopped, as if giving the ghosts time to disperse. Then she examined the quilt, and tears sprang to her eyes. "Kites," she said softly. "We just hold them by a string. I feel like that's all we have holding Pat now too."

Turning to the desk, she touched the frame on the Golden Surf. "I love this painting." She examined the family portrait. "Oh my, you'd certainly think from this picture that I'm a most unhappy person." She smiled. "That expression runs in my family. 'Old stern eyes,' my mother used to call me. Luckily, Pat didn't inherit it." One hand fluttered briefly at her neck. "Nor did Stephen." She opened the first desk drawer.

Within an hour, we'd been through every folder and envelope in Pat's desk and the two-drawer file cabinet. But turned up no Forester flyer. Marty arrived, announcing success at the registrar's office. "A.J. was in Pat's Advanced Comp class, spring of eighty six. I've got the roster in the car."

I updated him about Levere Eller's Bel Air. "What's the story on this assault?"

"Eller got an Incomplete in Pat's honors class. It's pretty hard not to pass honors — students set their own project guidelines. He didn't finish his project, tried a barrage of excuses. Even at that, she gave him right up to the day we filed grades to come through." He shrugged. "No project, no grade. The guy blew it. But he tried to bully her about it, right in the middle of the Student Union. He'd been drinking, and he tried to shove her. I shoved back. She complained to the Deans, and they suspended Eller, filed the charges just to be sure he'd stay off campus."

"You never had him in class, then?"

"No, but he told me I'd be sorry for playing White Knight."

"Is his name on that roster?"

"No."

"Why didn't you mention this before?"

He shrugged. "He was just a hot head kid, it was a while ago. It never occurred to me he might be involved in this."

Marty unlocked the basement storage room and carted up two boxes full of papers. Rose patiently sifted through them. Audrey Louise arrived after ferrying her kids from the matinee back to Aurora; she immediately began taking books off the shelves, shaking each of them, hoping the telltale pink would emerge. Rose asked if we'd like coffee — we opted for sodas. The sound of the ice in the glasses brought some cheer to the quiet of the apartment.

Rose asked Marty, "Would you show me some of Pat's photographs?"

He grinned. "Sure. We got some great shots when all of us went to Key West. That was the year before Ronnie died."

The memory stopped him. "Sorry," he said, tracing his beard at the jawline. "Ronnie was . . ."

"Your special friend?" Her eyes didn't waver from his face.

"Yes." He looked quickly at me, then selected a photo album from the bookshelf. Rose and I sat with him on the couch; Audrey Louise sat on the floor next to me. He flipped through pictures of Pat and Lou on a group camp-out — wimmin cooking together and canoeing, hiking arm-in-arm and laughing.

"Here they are at the Great Pink Boulder in upstate New York. Lou wrote a paper on ritual lodestones."

The Key West photos showed the smiling faces of two couples in love — at the beach, on the dance floor, lounging on the deck of a sailboat. "We ate shrimp till we were sick," Marty said, and laughed gently.

116

Rose ran her finger over one of Pat's photos. "She wore her hair like that when she was little. We called her Pixie." She leaned back against the couch. "My husband loved to take pictures, so we have shelves of albums. I remember one of Pat in a furry pink coat, taken when she was about six. She loved that coat so much that I couldn't get it off her to have it cleaned. One day in church she shocked us all by telling our minister that her coat had a name. She announced it proudly and loudly: Nipple."

None of us said a word. Then Rose started to laugh, and so did we. It felt good to finally let go.

"Too bad the Foresters chose pink for their flyers. It ruins a good color," Audrey Louise observed.

"Too bad we didn't find what we were looking for," Rose said with a sigh. Marty helped her take the glasses to the kitchen. She paused at the sink and touched a flamingo-shaped magnet on the refrigerator door. I picked up the album to put it away. As the photo sheets fell together, the elusive pink flyer floated to the carpet.

"Look!" Audrey Louse scooped it up.

"Is there a date?" Marty rushed over. "Oh, Pat, you Virgo-rising you, come through for us now!"

On the back of the cryptic note from the Sons of God, we all saw the small pencil mark at once. It read *5-22-86*.

We celebrated our victory all the way back to Aurora. So far our assumptions were on target. The links were there — the flyer sent at the same time that A.J. was in Pat's class, the same month that the Foresters had made their nasty debut. And the incident with Levere Eller had also occurred in May of '86. It remained to be seen how he could be connected to A.J.

117

Sandal's Jeep was parked in the Landry driveway. We found her stirring chili with Joel, while Gladdie and Tony pored over a large, yellowed tome on the table. "Your son insisted we go to the library," she told us. "But I welcomed it. Gladdie was about to purchase a set of King Edward chairs. Fit for a king, and at a king's ransom."

"What couldn't wait, honey?" Audrey Louise asked, examining the book over Tony's shoulder. *History of Brickmaking in the United States.*"

He blushed. "Well, I wanted to help Nyla."

"Anything about Colorado bricks?" I asked, touching his hair.

"Not really," Gladdie answered. "How'd things turn out on your end?"

Marty described our search for the flyer and the coinciding dates we'd discovered. "And Compoz has a promising lead on the car."

"Hey, all right!" Tony slapped a page of the history book. "They oughta have these now. We need 'em." He turned the book around to show me a photo of a brick inscribed with the words DON'T SPIT ON THE SIDEWALK. "I hate when guys do that," he said with a grimace. "Some guys do it all the way home. They *practice* spitting."

"Our non-spitter," Joel said, spooning out chili for us to taste. Marty started retelling Rose's story about Pat and the fuzzy pink coat, but in my mind, Bead's voice kept intoning, "K,L . . . K,L." Joel laughing about the coat named Nipple made me think of the mason's sense of humor — reversing letters just for the heck of it. K,L . . . K,L — what if *these* letters were reversed, and meant to be L,K? As in SIDEWALK. That would explain the letters being blocked out with a mold rather than carved into the clay free-hand.

"Great chili," Marty gasped, rushing to the sink. "Give me water!"

I rushed through the bricks book index to locate the date for the photograph Tony had singled out. The reference read: *Based on an ordinance passed in various states in the early 1900s."*

In the final hours before sunset, I swam slow laps in the pool. And realized that my dream about Lou and the barrel of floating pink flyers had been prescient — the one in the album had fallen from a page holding an intense portrait of her, as if she could indeed read the Forester message.

I hadn't been able to reach Compoz, so I'd have to wait for news on the Bel Air. Would it have the front fender dent? Could the police lab match the paint and rust? Could we find out if Eller knew A.J.? And how on earth could I pinpoint a date for the second set of pink notes? We had more questions than answers, but for the first time, I felt we had something.

Marty came down from the apartment. "I've been looking over this roster again." He sat down and dangled his feet in the water. "I do recognize one name. Bob Ross — he was in the paper a couple of months ago. Cited for his work in state social services by the Colorado AIDS Project."

Aha, Gladdie would have said. I stroked over to the side of the pool. We'd just found our horse of a different color.

12
PALOMINOS

Since Pat's roster included phone numbers, I contacted Bob Ross on Sunday morning. He was just on his way to church, and agreed to meet me afterward. Audrey Louise had already called the brick museum in Pueblo when I went down to borrow the station wagon.

"They'll call back if those ordinance bricks were made in Colorado. Then we can locate the sites."

I drove into central Denver, managed to squeeze the wagon into a parking place at Ninth and Clarkson. I'd told Bob I'd be wearing a sweatshirt with *Burnton Badgers* on it so he could recognize me.

An organ spieled benediction out the doors of the Metropolitan Community Church. It made my day watching the parishioners emerge — wimmin holding hands and kissing, men in full leather laughing with men in business suits; gay mothers and fathers with their children, gay children with their parents. No one denied communion.

I was proud of Bob Ross the minute I saw him. No bureaucracy would ever fade him to beige. He'd bronzed and spiked his crewcut, and he bounced with energy from his black Nikes to his red-ticking shirt and jazzy yellow tie. We walked to an ice cream shop a few blocks from the church. Over Frozen Yogurt De-Light, he told me about himself.

"I'm a mole." He grinned. "I run Reagan's money maze, finding funds to help gay people."

"Is that like a lavender Robin Hood?"

"You got it. Right under Uncle Sam's nose."

I asked about his recent award.

"That was a coup. I know several of the senators . . ." He pushed up his neon-blue glasses. "And out of the goodness of their hearts . . ." Again he grinned. "And my ardent pleas . . . and a potential blackmail grapevine that you wouldn't believe, well, C.A.P. was included in a blanket appropriation that will keep them operational for a year. If they'd applied on their own, with the current political climate, they wouldn't have seen dime one."

He'd clearly found his mission in life. "It gets no press here, but Colorado social services is providing help for gay people — we have our homeless too, and our battered and abused."

122

"Including Pat Stevens." I explained what we knew so far, what we were guessing at, and asked if he remembered A.J. Farrell from Pat's class.

"Remember him, sure. We worked together on a research project. He had an extra heavy load that semester, so Professor Stevens suggested he combine a pre-law project with an assignment for her. I happened to have an outline that fit both, and I needed help. We were a perfect match." His eyes sparkled; he looked like a grown-up Pixie.

I said, "Tell me about the research project."

"We summarized Colorado law, with documented case studies, relating to discrimination against gays. In housing, employment, and state services. I wanted to present the true picture of our legal recourse in these matters."

"How did A.J. react to the subject matter? My impression is that he's no great liberal."

"He knew my rep ahead of time. I was president of GSA on campus. Gay Student Activists."

"I'm still surprised."

"We interviewed nearly a hundred people. Bikers, nellies, radical dykes, corporate Amazons, Lesbian Moms, AIDS patients. He never balked. I think there are two things A.J. takes very seriously: his law studies and fitting in at the TKE house."

"You ever meet any of his frat buddies?"

Bob sighed loudly. "Only one. And I wish I hadn't. Robin Gaither. A.J. and I conducted most of our interviews at the GLCC. More than once, Gaither showed up there and they argued. He wanted A.J. to split. I think A.J. was embarrassed — by Gaither's actions, and probably about being at the Center himself."

123

"That didn't bother you?"

"I'm used to it. Besides, A.J. has a sensitive side. It's buried, but it's there."

"Any chance he's latent?"

Bob flipped his yellow tie at me. "That would only be wishful thinking. He's just had the bad taste to choose a best friend who's a jerk off."

"There's a campus rumor that Gaither buys his grades."

"That's more than a rumor. I have a buddy who paid for his car by writing Robin's papers." He pulled at his spikey bangs. "One thing I've always been able to do, Nyla, and that's network. You gotta start young."

"Guess it works for you in social services."

"And for A.J. too. One of my contacts got him that apprenticeship on the *Law Review*. He's impressing hell out of them, though. He works overtime — weekends, and nights. Since I'm on Sherman Street, I see his car in the Capitol lot all the time. I thought I kept long hours — he's showing me up."

Before we parted, I asked Bob for a copy of the project and a list of the people interviewed.

"Those names are confidential. Can't you tell me what you're looking for?"

"I could if I knew. But I'm following a chain of names and faces unknown to me, purely guessing at how they link up."

He relented and said he'd leave the list for me Monday at the GLCC.

More than anything, I wanted to talk with Compoz about Levere Eller. But since I was in the neighborhood, I stopped by Category Six, hoping Tell Parker might have caught up with Crazy Mary. From the street I could see the entire guild sunning themselves on the porch.

"It's that newspaper lady," Coral whispered as I came up the steps. Tell Parker had a copy of *The Advocate* shielding her eyes. She sat up slowly, closing the magazine.

"Lo, Nyla. Cops find that car yet?"

"I hope to hear something today."

"Parks Patrol have cooled their jets. Guess your guy took care of it."

I nodded. We all stood in the sunlight. Scout rolled up her bandanna and flicked it into the trees, breaking off twigs.

"Is Crazy Mary still upset about what happened the other day? Have you seen her?"

"Not hide nor hair of her," Gracie answered. Coral giggled, and P.D. flexed her leather glove.

"Maybe she flew up into one of those trees," Scout snarled.

Though I didn't expect Compoz to draw Sunday duty, I found him reared back at his desk, one battered tennis shoe cocked over the other. Frowning hard at a mug shot. His rose and lemon shirt belonged on a golf course.

"I hope you have a Bel Air ready to serve up on a silver platter."

His black eyes sparked. I could smell hair pomade and burned coffee. He shrugged. "Sorry, platter's still empty."

"Eller turned up legit?"

"Eller didn't turn up, period. The address we got from D.C.C. is his mother's. She claims he's been in Indiana working as a farmhand since before the hit-and-run. As for the car, he sold it to an uncle who owns a salvage yard in Grand Junction. She showed us the sales receipt."

"Oh god," I groaned, and slumped into a chair. "Back to square one."

"Yeah." He checked his coffee cup, grimaced at what he saw in it. Offered me some on his way for a refill. When he came back, I asked, "So what's your new plan?"

He propped his feet on his desk. "Go over everything again. See what we missed."

"Starting with A.J. Farrell," I said, and laid out our common denominator logic. Including the Forester flyer we'd found at Pat's, and what I'd learned from Bob Ross.

"I see your point about timing. But how are we going to find out when the new notes started?"

"I'm not sure yet. I just know if we can tie it up like we did the first ones, it's too much coincidence to ignore."

He worked his neck and chugged his coffee. "Maybe. Here's some more coincidence for you. Mrs. Eller is muchos mad about sonny boy's suspension. She's convinced Pat and Marty had it in for him. According to her, Levere was well on his way to college success before they ruined his chances. Including membership in a campus fraternity. The TKEs."

From the sergeant's office I called the apartment. When no one answered, I dialed the main house. Joel informed me that my escapades had sent his wife flying off to the brick museum in Pueblo. "Marty and the boys went with her. So I'm here all alone. Except for the dancing girls, of course." He was still laughing at his own joke when I hung up.

* * * * *

126

The Capitol thrust up its golden breast to the afternoon sun. A.J.'s convertible sucked in the heat like a small red planet. Several other cars were parked nearby, but certainly the lot had a different character from its night-time persona. The Grand Back Door was unlocked; I entered at the second level and walked directly into the gallery above the senate floor. The space seemed small for the momentous decisions of state, the filibusters, senatorial quarrels about quarantine and gun control, budgets and capital punishment. I heard footsteps in the hall.

"Can I help you, Miss?" A matronly guard rested a hand on her holster."

"I'm looking for the *Law Review* office."

"That's in the basement. I'll show you."

A.J. sat at a typewriter; two other men worked on layout at the far end of the room. The guard closed the door behind me, and A.J. turned. Brimming with his usual high energy, he bounced up to greet me. "Nyla, what's up? How'd you find me?"

"You said you were busting butt over here. I came to see for myself."

Suddenly he lost his smile. "Has something happened with Pat?"

"No, take it easy. I just wanted to talk to you about one of your frat brothers. Levere Eller — he was involved in assault charges. Pat filed the complaint."

A.J. turned back to his desk. "Man, you scared me. I thought maybe she'd developed complications. I guess I should be thinking she's gonna come out of it any minute, shouldn't I?" He looked at me as if I'd never mentioned Eller.

"So do you know this guy? Compoz says he's a TKE."

"Before my time, maybe. I don't know him."

127

His voice didn't quite convince me. "You never heard about the assault then?"

He shook his head. "I must be in some ivory tower, huh? I miss all the good stuff." He grinned, but moved his eyes back to his papers.

I hadn't expected this glitch in logic. I thought of Compoz covering the same old ground again. "A.J., when did you and Pat start running together? Was it right after she moved in?"

He rubbed one shoulder. "I noticed right away she was an ambitious runner. But it took about three months to get up my nerve to ask if we could run together."

"So that would have been . . ."

"Uh, September of last year. She moved in in July."

"Lately, though, say in the last three months or so, you didn't notice any change in mood, maybe a change in her running pattern?"

He walked over to the typewriter, glanced at what he'd written. "Like I told you before, we didn't talk that much about personal stuff. Pat almost never missed her runs. Unless she was sick — that's about the only time I remember her not going out. For about a week in March, I guess it was, she had the flu." He chuckled. "I had to run through that snow in the Gauntlet by myself. Man, I missed her. She sorta egged me on, you know?"

He waited for more questions. I'd run out of steam. "Thanks, A.J. Hope I didn't interrupt your work too much."

"No problem. I'd do anything to help Pat."

As I started toward the door, the image of the blond boy flashed in my mind. "Working late and all, I suppose you've noticed the action in the parking lot."

128

I expected his ready grin, but he stared at me without smiling. "I never stay past six-thirty. I'm outta here before the chickens come to roost."

As I sat in the Landry station wagon on Grant Street, with the waning sun molding a sticky Twinkie wrapper into the dashboard, I re-ran my conversation with A.J. He'd lied — about Eller, and his hours at the Capitol. But had it been deliberate? He'd have to leave the *Law Review* office soon to meet with his Torts tutor, unless that was also a lie. Or unless someone on the *Law Review* staff served as his tutor. That, at least, would be easy enough to confirm.

Something else intrigued me — *chickens* — he knew that word for underage prostitutes. But maybe everyone at the Capitol knew it. Maybe I was clinging to straws and too many maybes. I put the key in the ignition — then decided to stick around a little longer.

By seven o'clock, the red convertible began to bleed into the shadows of the trees. I walked down to a 7-11 and bought a bag of junk food, and went back to my lonely vigil. By eight-thirty, the clouds behind the dome were gunmetal grey, edged with black just over the mountains. One by one, the boys walked in, swaggering in ragged jeans, flicking cigarettes like fireflies into the falling darkness.

With my window down, I could hear them laughing, making animal calls. Screeching out, "Hey wildcat!" "Hey foxbait!" "Hot time tonight, babe." The sun had not yet surrendered when the line of cars began. The blond boy perched on a ledge by the steps, but never came

129

down to do any business. Maybe he's just a sightseer himself tonight, I thought.

When night finally swallowed the dome's gold, the circling cars blurred into a stream of moving lights like a lantern underwater. The other men from the *Law Review* were long gone. Staring at the dark blot of the convertible, my eyes burned; I longed for a night scope like the cops use on bunko stings. I ate a chocolate bar, caramel corn, a package of cookies, and washed it down with a soda. Shortly, I dozed into sugar blitz.

"Be careful, Darren."

The friendly warning jerked me awake — the blond boy was waving to a skinny black kid in a beret as he got into a Cadillac with three other men. I squinted into the night to see if the convertible was still there.

The blond left the steps, walked to the fountain, and repeated his ritual splashing. He seemed to be waiting. Was there a special car coming for him? He turned into the shadows away from the fountain, away from the steps. A circling car honked. "Beat it!" he yelled, leaning for just one moment into a slash of light from the streetlamps, where another blond joined him, and they headed for the red car.

13
ROLLING STONES

So the pre-law frat man led a double life — and he obviously cared a great deal about concealing it. It was clear why he'd lied about his Sunday nights, but not about his hours at the Capitol. Surely working there gave him a perfect smoke screen. Could there be an innocent explanation? He and the prostitute were childhood friends. Maybe they just went bowling. Maybe he was trying to help the blond out of the life in the Shallows.

Hell, the kid could be part of a new class project. Somehow I couldn't convince myself.

Night was quiet in Aurora; Audrey Louise and Joel cuddled in a double lounger by the pool and talked with Marty. "We thought maybe we'd lost you," Marty said when I joined them.

Audrey Louise snapped a towel in my direction. "We got worried. You've been gone all day."

Marty handed me a beer. "Sandal and Gladdie are planning to be up all night working on the Amazon. They'd like us to come to the studio. Drink wine, talk politics, bolster the creative urges."

Joel got up, pulling Audrey Louise with him. "You've had my wife on the chase enough for one day. I'd like a little time with her myself." They headed for the house.

"You find out about the bricks?" I called after them.

"Nothing startling. We'll go over it in the morning."

Marty stood up. "So shall we foray to Lookout Mountain?" When I didn't answer, he added, "This will be like old times. Reviling the powers that be. Dreaming of future powers. Watching art birth itself." He studied me a moment. "What's on your mind, Nyla? You look like you've had the wind knocked out of your sails."

"Maybe we all have." I stretched, thought about staying awake for hours. Thought about the Amazon. I wanted to see her emerge. "Come on, let's head up to the studio. You drive. I'll talk."

On the road up the mountain, night cupped itself against the black breast of the cliffs, the headlights pushing only a thin one-way tunnel into the darkness. I felt as if we were driving inside a Chinese finger puzzle. I described my stakeout at the Capitol to Marty. "You

132

think there's another explanation for A.J.'s connection with the prostitute?"

"Sounds like real dalliance to me. Unless the blond is a relative."

"What if we've figured A.J. wrong? Who knows what he might do to stay in his closet. Especially if he's our pipeline to the Foresters."

"I thought you saw him as an unwitting stoolie."

"I was guessing."

We headed toward a barn-like building with light streaming out across the dirt driveway. Odd-shaped humps of stone in a sideyard loomed like night-huge gremlins. Marty honked the horn in three short bursts. "My signal," he said with a chuckle. "So Gladdie doesn't come out with her shotgun blazing."

Inside the studio was a jumbled hive of mid-birth art, life trying to get out of stone. Here and there partial faces, a webbed hand, a breast with a daisy at the nipple, the soft round thrust of a buttock. Huge logs on sawhorses could become a canoe or a totem. Wads of wet clay squatted on boards. Mounds of dry clay cracked like big brown eggs, perhaps they would spill out baby dinosaurs, odd little creatures to scurry around the tall, legged metal forms everywhere awaiting parts.

"No welcoming committee, that's strange." Marty scouted the maze toward the back of the studio. Called for Sandal and Gladdie as he moved toward a raised, circular platform, on it a half-covered block of stone as tall as the studio doors. I reconnoitered the jumble of logs and potter's tables, trying to keep up with him.

"Sandal! Hey, Gladdie! Where are you?" His voice reverberated in the huge shed. "We've come for the all-nighter. Bring on Bacchus!" He reached the large stone at the back. "Good god! What happened here?"

I clambered over the big riser. The cloth covering the sculpture had been slashed away. Sandal's Amazon brandished a spear, but the giant warrior had taken a beating. Someone had sledge-hammered her, demolishing her chin, pulverizing a shoulder, battering a breast away. In red spray paint across the damaged stone was the word LEZ, and a crude drawing of a pine tree.

We raced back through the clutter to the house, but it was dark and empty. Marty flashed the car lights out into the trees and bore down on the horn. Then we listened. Heard two small booms pumped against the air — both barrels of a shotgun.

"The quarry road!" he shouted and jumped into the car. I leaped in after him, and we peeled out of the driveway with the passenger door flapping. The little Toyota jittered, gears grinding, back wheels fishtailing a cloud of gravel. We nearly went off the road in the loose dirt. The headlights scanned nothing but tall grass and empty road. No sign of Sandal or Gladdie.

Suddenly tail lights flashed up ahead, disappearing red dots a quarter of a mile away. Someone limped along the side of the road. Marty screeched to a halt as the figure rolled into the ditch.

"Sandal, it's Marty. Sandal!" In the dark, he stumbled over the shoulder of the road and nearly fell into the ditch on top of her. I scrambled after them, and heard Gladdie call out of the darkness.

"She okay?"

"I think so."

Down in the ditch, Sandal looked dazed; Marty propped his arm behind her shoulders. "Sonsabitches got away," she mumbled, spitting dirt and rubbing her elbow. "I just about had 'em, only I hit the new cut at the tree line and nearly broke my neck."

"How many were there?" I wished for a flashlight.

"I saw two."

Gravel showered down on us as Gladdie rumbled into the ditch. "You okay, hon? They hurt you?" She reached for Sandal, and brushed at her face.

"Hell, I hurt myself trying to catch up to them. They must be track stars."

"You hit anyone?" Marty asked, eyeing the shotgun.

"No, I just wanted to scare them."

"How many did you see?" I asked her.

"Two, but not close up."

Sandal leaned her head on Gladdie's breast. "Did you see what they did to my stone? Sonsabitches bashed in one of her breasts."

Gladdie stroked her hair. Starlight flashed off her gun barrel. "She'll be all right."

"Hell yes," Marty confirmed. "She's an Amazon."

Back at the studio, I put in a call to Compoz. Gladdie daubed at Sandal's scrapes with a washcloth. Marty made tea that we laced with whiskey. Within thirty minutes, the sergeant and a uniformed officer pulled into the drive.

"Everyone okay?" Compoz asked.

"Everyone except the Amazon," Sandal answered angrily.

The sergeant walked slowly through the maze of the studio back to the stone on the platform. "Get some photos," I heard him say. His footsteps echoed off the ceiling, off the metal manikins and lumps of clay as he rejoined us. "Tell me what happened."

We had a quick story for him. Sandal and Gladdie took a late dinner break at 10:30. Came back from the house about 11:15, heard noise at the back of the studio. Sandal chased the vandals through the trees; Gladdie headed them off on the road. Neither had been close enough to see faces, hair color, anything. And we'd only seen the retreating tail lights.

In the cavernous studio, Compoz closed his small leather notebook with a quiet snap. "I doubt they'll be back," he said. "But just in case, the officer will stay at the end of your driveway awhile." He looked at me. "Guess they didn't go back underground after all."

My dreams were a blur of stone chips and flying hammers, golden horses with fiery hooves, wimmin warriors falling in battle. A rerun of that moment in the lamplight when I saw A.J. join the blond boy. I was glad to wake up, to give up wondering what specter rode that horse and wielded that hammer. It was Monday, and I set out to wield my best energy in solving the mystery that bound us all.

I snagged Marty about to step into the shower. Gave him a mission back to the registrar's office to verify Eller's membership in the TKEs, and to see if Pat had cancelled any classes in March. Next I called Gene Nile to let him know about Bob Ross's list of interviewees. "I'd appreciate your reading it over. I'm not sure what we're looking for. Maybe you can tell me." Then I headed for the main house to tell Audrey Louise about the attack on the Amazon, and to get her report on the bricks.

She poured us both coffee, shaking her head. "This has got to stop, it just has to."

"We're about to plug the leak. Not many people knew what Sandal was working on, but she did tell A.J. So everything points back to him. I wonder just how

136

innocent a pipeline he is, considering some of his friendships." I told her about his connection in the Shallows.

"This gets more convoluted by the minute. I'm glad I've got the simplicity of searching out bricks. The womon at the museum was most helpful. She showed us the repress machine, and talked to us about the frogs. They're like brands really — no two exactly alike, even the ones done in a mold."

"So what about a sites map?"

"I've got a name at the state building commission. I'll go this morning right after I feed the troops." Who promptly marched into the kitchen, cranky from sleep and demanding full ration.

After my own shower, I phoned the studio. It took ten rings till Gladdie answered, breathless.

"Not out chasing vandals again, I hope?"

"No, helping sandblast the Amazon. At least we got the red paint off."

"Can you salvage her?"

"You know Sandal, she doesn't give up easily. And she's decided a warrior without scars is hardly credible." The laughter in her voice assured me that Sandal had the best help in the world.

"Before the attack, you sensed nothing out of the ordinary?"

"Actually I did. Sort of a jittery feeling in the early evening. But sometimes when things are too close to home, I shield myself from knowing. After all, if we'd come into the studio sooner, we might have been physically harmed."

"I'm just thankful they ran instead of standing to fight. My money would have been on you two, though, with the shotgun and the sledgehammer."

"Tag-team bravery, I assure you."

"I wondered if you'd go with Audrey Louise to check out these brick sites. We may need your special expertise, especially if most of the bricks have been removed."

"Like a rolling stone," Gladdie teased. "Humor, Nyla, I hope to Goddess it carries us through all this. Of course I'll help with the bricks."

Marty reported in from the campus. "Levere Eller was an active TKE member at the time the assault charges were filed. I checked with the fraternity sponsor — Eller's house privileges weren't revoked till the end of spring eighty-six semester. But Nyla, why are we checking on Eller? If he sold his car and he was out of state —"

"Then why did A.J. lie and say he didn't know him? Unless something about Eller is connected, and it puts a bad light on the fraternity. It's a piece in the puzzle. What about Pat's sick time?"

"Two days off in March. The eighth and ninth."

By lunch time, Audrey Louise was ready to go to the building commission where Gladdie would meet her. I wanted to shag one of the police photos of the Amazon and crank up some prose about the Forester's latest public relations. Spin by the GLCC and have a look at that list. And maybe visit A.J. Farrell.

On my way to the Center, I pondered those two days Pat took off in March. She'd had the flu, A.J. said, didn't run for a week. She'd gone back to the classroom, but stayed out of the Gauntlet. Something about the timing stuck in my thoughts.

Busy phones rang at the GLCC; a girl who looked barely out of her teens tried to handle the inquiries. She took her work seriously. I wondered what it would have been like had I known I was a lesbian at her age. Gene conferred with a group of men gathered in a small meeting room just off the main entrance. He waved. "Be with you in a sec."

I browsed the bookshelves until he ushered me into his office.

"Sorry, it's always crazy Monday morning. We have our AIDS patients and support group, so the day often starts with sad news. We're keeping a scrapbook. We write goodbye notes to the friends we've lost." He handed me an envelope. "Here's your list."

"You get any great visions from it?"

"Tell you the truth, I didn't have time. If you let me make a copy, I'll look it over in more detail later. But this morning is just too rushed."

"Sure, I understand." I looked at the envelope, then back at Gene. "How many? Have you lost?"

"One was more than I ever wanted to count," he said.

I was hungry; I wanted Nubian breast cake and simpler times. I grabbed some fast food hash browns and pulled into the Capitol lot. Colorado politicians are prompt; every parking space was taken. I drove up Sherman Street, sent a positive thought to Bob Ross the government mole, and wedged in on the bumper of a Mercedes coupe.

The senate gallery was already closed; I missed my buxom guard. Bet she was a crack shot, probably kept a speedloader in her bouffant, smoked a pack a day, liked a whack of scotch now and then. Loved the subtle action here under the dome. I found my own way back to the *Law Review* office.

Inside, only one bright face awaited visitors. The womon, her glasses up in her hair and a pencil clamped in her mouth, reminded me of my editor. Serious attention to detail. "Can I help you?"

"I was hoping to talk to a friend of mine. A.J. Farrell?"

"Sure, I know him. But he won't be in until this afternoon."

"Do you know what time? I need his help. I'm having trouble with one of my pre-law classes."

She allowed a quick smile. "Well, I'm a senior at D.C.C. so I know the program pretty well. What year are you?"

"Sophomore. But I just changed majors. I got into this Torts class, and I'm drowning. What I need is a tutor. Since A.J. has one, I was hoping to horn in."

She pulled her glasses down for a closer look at me. "A.J. has a tutor for Torts? Are you sure? He's an honors level student. Everyone wants *him* to tutor *them*."

"Geez, I thought maybe someone here was helping him."

"Not that I know of. I don't think any of the law profs even offer tutoring. It's almost bad politics. Half of pre-law is bluff, looking cool under fire. We're all headed for courtrooms; we have to show the right stuff."

Just to be on the safe side, I called Marty from the pay phone in the rotunda. Asked him to venture back to the registrar's office one more time. "I want to be sure we've tracked this tutor deal completely."

"I know the pre-law department head. I'll check with him."

"No tutor, no alibi," I said to myself as I hung up.

140

* * * * *

We were trying to turn every stone, I thought as I drove to the police building. I wondered how Audrey Louise and Gladdie were doing with the bricks. Wondered if Pat dreamed in her coma. Wondered if Lucy dreamed about me.

The Sergeant wasn't at his desk. I waited on a bench outside the door, listened to the hum of phones and voices. Smelled waves of cologne as men in shirt sleeves came by, their holsters bulging like extra muscles. I heard Compoz in the hallway: "Sanders, you and Copek roll on this domestic out on Federal." He glanced at me, marched on into his office. "Come in and shut the door behind you."

I sat down. "You're getting a rep for catering to reporters?"

His dark, flat eyes told me this was no day for jokes. "I know what you want." He tossed me a folder. "These just came from the photo lab. Pick out a couple for your story." Pictures of the battered Amazon.

"Thanks." I went over them slowly, to give his mood a little space. He rummaged around his desk, then pushed back in the chair and propped up his feet — lizard-skin boots with copper toe-caps. "I went back out to Sandal Morgan's this morning," he said, squeaking the leather of one boot against the other. "Just to look around. See if anything snagged in the trees." He kicked his boots down and opened a desk drawer. Slung a plastic evidence pouch on the desk. It held a black stocking cap. "Hanging like a flag on a lower branch." He poked it with one finger. "We got a few strands of hair in it. Blond."

I felt a flood of too much coincidence. A.J. and the blond together last night. Then two vandals up at the

141

studio, and blond hair in the stocking cap. But why would he do it? Unless he needed to bolster his smoke screen. Or unless he was a full player. I told Compoz about my stakeout.

"Adds a new twist, all right." He rubbed his belt buckle. "But we've still got no proof. Damn, I wish we could turn just one element on this case. Get some momentum." He looked at me, sighed loudly. "At the risk of spooking him, I'll think about having a chat with Mr. Farrell. Or we could pick up the kid — they don't want trouble with the cops. He might be pretty willing to talk. Meantime, we got a nasty home fight going in north Denver, three B and Es with battery, and an Aggravated. And the day's just begun."

Resisting the urge to have my own chat with A.J. proved impossible. Since he didn't know that I was onto him, maybe I could find out his whereabouts last night. See what tales he'd tell to cover his tracks from the Shallows. By the time I pulled up to the sixplex, I'd decided on my angle. I'd ask if he thought there might be a way to trace the Bel Air via the vintage car network. Associations, special body shops, any particular salvage yards where he'd scrounged parts for the Merc. Get him talking about his car, get him relaxed, get him to tell me what I wanted to know.

He didn't answer the bell, so I knocked. I realized chances were slim I'd catch him here in between classes. Still, I went around to the back to see if the Merc was there. The car sparkled red greeting. Not a trace of quarry road dust, I noticed, but he'd had time to wash it. When I knocked on the back door, I found it ajar.

"A.J.? It's Nyla Wade," I called into the empty kitchen. I went toward the living room, hoping Monday wasn't A.J.'s morning to sleep in. At the doorway, I stopped. As before, the grey leather couch on the rose rug looked intimate and inviting. But the coffee table had met destruction, the amber glass smashed away from the chrome frame in huge chunks. As if someone had put his foot down.

I called again for A.J. Stepped quickly past the shattered pile of glass to glance into the bedroom and bathroom. The apartment was deserted and intact except for this small demolition in the living room. On closer look, I found the torn pieces of a photograph amid the glass. These I collected before I split.

Back in the station wagon, I pieced together the puzzle of the torn picture. A Polaroid with bad contrast, but I knew the face. He was nude, playing nature boy against the backdrop of spring-bright aspen and the ruins of a mountain cabin. The blond boy once again.

Some bizarre scenario had taken place in A.J.'s apartment. I couldn't begin to guess at it, nor to guess how I could ask him about it. Who broke the table? Who tore up the photo? Who argued so violently on the rose rug, and who won the fight?

Down the block in front of the sixplex a moving form took shape, and I felt a sudden wash of relief. Delivery was at hand. For a moment I was back in time, two years ago in front of the Shady Stay Motel in Burnton, Oregon, when a red-headed postwoman had nearly bowled me over. And had since stolen my heart. Now another womon moved down the street toward me, rolling with the weight of the big leather shoulder bag and threading letters between her fingers. Her blue shirt signaled a spot of hope in this day, I knew it.

143

I caught up with her and squinted into the sunlight. "Going to be a hot walk today."

She smiled. "Yes, but I've got a short shift, so it's okay."

"Oh, this isn't your regular route?" My balloon of hope began to deflate.

"No, but I've covered it often enough. The regular had a baby in January. So she's been off a lot."

"Mostly college kids around here?" We were three houses from the sixplex.

"Quite a few. Turn over's high enough. Means FWDs to keep track of."

I knew from Lucy that this meant forwarding notices.

She dug in the bag for a wad of catalogs. "This guy's an astronomy nut. Gets telescope parts all the time. Man, I hate to lug these." She grinned, and pointed across the street. "Couple lives over there, they must be learning Arthur Murray. I always have records for them. Carry those a couple miles, you don't feel like dancing." She shook her head, still smiling. "I hardly ever see any of these people, but I know them all."

"Any brown-paper-wrapper types?" I grinned back at her, familiar with all of this shop talk from living with my own personal postwoman.

She laughed. "One old man orders a lot from Eve's Garden."

I laughed. We walked together toward the sixplex. "Let me ask you something. I've got a friend in this building, and she's been receiving . . . well, some real unwelcome mail. As in threatening notes. What's weird is, they all came on pink paper." I realized what a complete long shot it was to expect the carrier to remember pink notes at a particular address. But she seemed familiar enough with the route and like Compoz said, you had to ask. "We never found any envelopes, but she received quite a few of the notes. Probably within the last month or so."

"Which apartment? Wait a sec, that lady runner, I bet."

"You read about her in the paper?"

"No, I just remember her because she's always running. Morning and night. Man, even in winter when it was icy and sleeting. Sometimes she'd do her stretch work out here." The carrier shifted her bag again. "Pink envelopes. No, I sure don't remember any. You could check with the regular, I suppose. And I'd alert the postal inspector too. He could watch for any pink notes from now on." She looked down at her handful of letters. "Sorry she's had this trouble."

She went up the steps to the row of mailboxes. I'd drawn a pitiful blank in trying to discover the timing of the second set of notes. The carrier finished, wished me a good day, and walked on past. Then she turned back. "You know, one day this winter that lady was out here in her sweats. Getting ready for her run like always. I told her how great it was nothing stopped her. She sort of laughed, then surprised me by taking her mail back inside. I remember what she said. 'Nothing stops me but the Ides of March.'"

146

14

HOPE ON A HIGH WIRE

The postwomon had come through — the timing fit. Ides of March included the seven days preceding the 15th. Putting the focus on the 8th and 9th — those two days when Pat had cancelled her classes. The week she didn't run with A.J. because he thought she had the flu. She had a case of something, all right. My guess was fear, because the new notes had started. So drastically different in tone from the first set: *Out of the closet, into a coffin.* No wonder Pat had the jitters and stayed close to home.

147

I headed for the CNB office to file my story. Found Bead scowling over the teletype as if none of the news satisfied her. I waved the Amazon photos at her. "Latest Forester scoop: sledgehammer attack."

It was tough not to editorialize about the vandalism, tough not to paint a picture of how it felt zigging down that country road in the dark, terrified that the vandals had taken their hammers to the sculptor. And more, I wanted to write something astute about what happens when fear and ignorance ignite inside the human mind. Something about the hammer of God belonging in God's domain. I knew Bead would strike every subjective word. The phone buzzed.

"Nyla, it's Audrey Louise. We've seen Denver from all angles today. Fronts and backs of government buildings. Bricks and brick piles."

"My eternal gratitude. You come up with anything?"

"The ordinance bricks were laid in front of all new government buildings that year. Of twelve sites, eight have been rebuilt or refurbished. The bricks were destroyed."

"Any chance of them being recycled, hauled somewhere, left at the edge of a dump?"

"Ground to brick dust, we have the word of state government. None were incinerated, so those traces of soot remain a mystery."

"What about the other four?"

"Original bricks still in place. We went to see for ourselves, Gladdie wanted to be sure none of them had ever been replaced. It's possible some could've been used for private homes, but that's unlikely. No records would be available anyway. So for our purposes, all the bricks are accounted for."

I sighed. "Another dead end." More almost-clues, like the blond hair in the stocking cap. "Thanks anyway. I'll see you back at the house."

"We're headed over to Presbyterian first, to see if Rose will take a break. Do a mall crawl, or maybe just go out for lunch."

I suggested Patience and Sarah's.

After the day's mixture of events, I realized I'd have the apartment and the pool to myself. The thought was tempting — a long swim, baking in the sun a few hours. Maybe I'd call Lucy and see how the home fires were burning. Peel away a layer of our non-communication. Hell, just tell her I loved her. She knew it, but there are times when saying the words is essential.

Instead, I drove toward the D.C.C. campus, some vague plan forming at the back of my brain.

Stuck between the press of metro Denver and the granite of the Rockies hogback, the campus buildings hunkered down on the buffalo grass like a dare: to winters and smog and the greater prestige of Denver University. To tight budgets and closure threats. To the prejudice that a smaller college means smaller opportunity, or small mindedness. My old school loyalty was showing, but I knew if I had any courage in me, I'd learned it here.

Unsure where the TKE house was located, I drove the few blocks' radius of the campus. Found the Alpha Gams and Delta Sigs before I spotted the sign on the big white two-story. Out in front, coeds played touch football. I didn't see A.J. or Robin.

I turned up the alley and drove behind the house, pulling up next to a new silver Baretta parked behind a brick garage. I knew even as I stepped out of the car that it would be difficult to get anything out of A.J. with his frat buddies around. Especially about what had happened at his apartment.

I glanced through the narrow door of the garage, which was really an old carriage house, expecting to see maybe storage boxes and a sprung couch, but nothing in particular.

Certainly not the flair of green fins knifing through the dust.

The huge car nearly burst the walls of the carriage house. I noticed immediately that both front fenders had rusted through; for all its chrome, the grille looked like a dragon's maw. Pushing my way around stacks of yellowed newspapers and a pile of boards, I examined the front of the car carefully. Ran my hand along the passenger-side bumper, and felt a half-moon dent inward. Saw the new crease like a fresh welt in the metal. Right under our noses — I could hardly believe it. Until I found the model logo. Not a '66 Bel Air.

I brushed off my hands, stood looking at the car in disgust. I remembered A.J. telling us about this car, the Imperial that Robin wouldn't get restored. There must be any number of explanations for the dent, probably something as innocent as hitting a tree stump at a beer bust. Then I thought about Dugan's lecture on guesswork and luck. Everything we had on this case so far was a long-shot guess or a near-miss idea. Even the I.D. on the Bel Air was the best guess of Covelli the auto salvager. Could there be any chance that he'd guessed wrong? Just in case, I used a screwdriver to flake a few paint chips off the front bumper into a tissue.

* * * * *

In a moment's sun-blindness as I stepped out of the garage, I blundered into Robin Gaither. His load of books splayed at his feet. "You lost in traffic?" he teased, pointing to the old car.

"Looking for A.J.," I mumbled. "I went to his apartment and the back door was open, but he wasn't there." I saw a quick change in Robin's bronzed cheeks. Then he curled his lips back off his straight white teeth in what passed for a smile.

"Haven't seen him at all today. You were in his apartment, you say?"

"Yes." For some reason, I didn't mention the coffee table.

He picked up his books. "I saw your article in the *Post.* This Foresters business is pretty bizarre. I thought the only Nazi-conservative types were in church. Anything new happening?"

"See tonight's edition. Remember that sculpture Sandal Morgan told us she was working on? Someone took a sledgehammer to it."

"Jesus, how could anyone . . ." He shaded his eyes from the sun. "But then, if these same people ran Professor Stevens down with a car . . ."

"There's no proof of that, I'm afraid. Or anything else, for that matter. But at least the police are staying on the case."

"How is Professor Stevens?"

"Still in a coma."

He shook his head. "Sleeping death," he said, hefting the books in his arms.

"Where you off to? A used book sale?" I grinned at him.

He laughed. "I wish. I'm going to the library. Have to finish up my honors project."

His words reminded me of the incident with Levere Eller. "You mind my asking about one of your frat brothers? The police wanted to question him about Pat Stevens because of an old assault charge."

Robin leaned his books on the hood of the Baretta. Cocked his eyes at me, and kept his body language loose. But I felt a sudden tension. "You mean Levere."

I nodded. He sighed, crossed his arms over his chest. "We thought he'd make it, even though he came in on academic probation. I liked him. We hung out together. But he couldn't hold his liquor. He drank too much too often. He blew it on the easy stuff."

"Eller got along okay with A.J.?"

"Sure, why not? He got along with everyone. But like I say, he was too much of a party guy."

"You stay in touch with him since he went to Indiana?"

Robin looked down at his tennis shoes. Waited a moment before he answered, "I guess I should have. But I didn't."

At least he acknowledged Eller; that was more than A.J. had been willing to do. "Honors class, I'm surprised. That doesn't fit with the reputation of wild toga parties and Animal House."

He grinned. "We do that too, but you have to make three point to stay active. So guys study hard, then we party hard. Not usually in town — we've got a special place out by Sandhorn Lake."

"Your own mountain clubhouse?"

"More like our own falling down shack. We fix it up just enough to keep it from caving in on us."

* * * * *

I went back to the campus and found Marty, who told me his activity of this day was finished. "If A.J. has a tutor, there's no record of it," he reported. I told him what my day had netted — all bricks accounted for, but not the coffee table. Not the torn photo nor the stocking cap. Not the Ides of March. "Whatever happened in March to start that new set of notes is linked to A.J. I'd bet my life on it."

"You better not have to." He put his arm around my shoulders. "You had lunch?"

We grabbed a burrito at Chubby's, a dilapidated Spanish diner that served up Denver's hottest tough-skinned Mexican food in greasy tissue wrappers. Fire eating, we'd always called it. Then we walked along the campus sidewalk past Kilty Hall, Bannock Tower, Milton Observatory, and back toward Pike School of Journalism. A breeze came up with a faint, plaintive wooing sound. "You been over to the hospital today?" I asked Marty.

"No, I was planning to go this evening. I'm sure Rose is exhausted, with nothing to do and no sign of change in Pat."

"Audrey Louise and Gladdie took her out for lunch."

My thoughts went to that night a week ago when Pat had walked into the living room in Aurora, so changed, and yet her spirit still the same in me, in my memory of her, as I held it now, waiting to offer it up for strength. *I remember your poem for Janis Joplin.* A poem I couldn't recall myself. It touched me to realize that we had carried a portion of each other in our lives, had used this energy in positive ways only now becoming clear to us. "Pat Stevens was the first fearless womon I ever met," I said.

*****

Marty headed out to Aurora; I made another stop at the DPD. Presented Compoz with my wadded-up tissue containing the Imperial paint samples.

"You really know how to spend the taxpayer's money," he grumped. "Spectrophotometry ain't cheap."

"If it matches up, won't it be worth it?" I gave him my most charming smile.

"Two days to get the pyrolysis right," he grumped again. "By then, the Foresters could drive that Bel Air to the high country and dump it off a cliff."

Steam flashed up from the grill when Marty added a splash of chablis to shrimp kabobs. "Just about perfect," he called from the deck. I tossed the salad and poured our dinner wine. The phone rang.

"The omnipresent beast," I said, and answered. Listened to words that stopped my heart. Heard the line buzz quickly. I tried to call to Marty, but my voice failed me. My heart kicked over and pounded in my ears. When he touched my arm, all I could say was, "Stack the shrimp. We've got to get to the hospital."

Sandal met us in the waiting room; Gladdie and Audrey Louise had gone for coffee. Rose was resting in a room nearby. "Dr. Powers gave her a light sedative."

"What the hell happened?" Marty blustered, running his hands over his beard, his eyes sparking with worry.

"Pat's having some kind of seizures. Dr. Powers thinks there's been a sudden pressure buildup on the brain. They're testing now for fluid. If that's causing the pressure, it will require surgery. But with the seizures, surgery would be too risky. So it's like double jeopardy."

154

"When did this start?" I asked.

"Six-thirty or so. She's been having the seizures about every twenty minutes. They're afraid to give her medication since she's in the coma. Same ole diagnosis — the only thing we can do is wait."

We waited together, in our little huddle of friends, sipping coffee and lighting cigarettes. A primal vigil, the only comfort our shared presence. Rose awakened and joined us, silent, unable to hide her fear. About ten-thirty, Gene Nile stepped off the elevator.

"I went out to your apartment, learned from the fellow in the main house what had happened."

After I introduced him to everyone, we took a walk to the sun gallery.

"Sorry to bother you at a time like this, Nyla, but I thought you'd want to know. I went over that list Bob Ross gave you and matched up two of the names. Seems they interviewed both the nurse and teacher who were later harassed by the Foresters."

It took me a moment to realize the implication. "In other words, that list was more than a source for their research project."

After Gene left, I sat in the gallery awhile. Closed my eyes and tried to open my mind for a clear view of our next move. Instead, I heard Pat's laughter, saw out of our past the prideful toss of her head, the brightness of will in her young eyes. Saw out of our present the turquoise lotus blossoms, and phrases from her poems. "Only a cloak of hope and a sword of love . . ."

It came to me that the sword of love is not forged of steel, has no cutting edge, is no weapon at all save surrender to faith, the heart laid upon an altar to higher power. We have no armor to wear in life except acceptance, hope, resilience. And we can only heal each other with unwavering love.

It was then that I remembered the poem I'd written for Janis Joplin.

> Janissoul, gut of fire and tears
> Your songs wail down from the thin air.
> Your tenuous life is a test
> Of hope on a high wire
> Moving hand over hand.

It was now a poem for Pat, and for all of us, hoping and waiting — our swords of love surrendered to the highest faith. I found a phone and called Lucy, to tell her I loved her.

15
CHARIOTS BEWARE

As each of us stood sentry at Pat's bedside, we thought the worst had come: delirium and tremors, as if she were chilled to the core and suffering fevers of the soul. Eventually Rose collapsed into exhausted sleep. None of us wanted to leave her alone, but we had to rest. For there would come another day's waiting — how many we didn't know.

Audrey Louise and I drove back to Aurora in silence. No energy to talk, no words to convey our feelings. We hugged in the driveway, and I climbed the steps to the apartment. Marty had dropped onto the couch, still in his clothes. I threw a blanket over him. The phone shrilled, loud as the hospital alarm monitors that had blared over Pat's bed. I grabbed the receiver.

The stranger had his say in quick hot words. Mean and scary and over in a moment. Shock paralyzed me. I held the phone, listening, waiting, even after he hung up. The message echoed in my ears.

"Queers are bearers of the plague. Stand up for them, go down with them. Next the hammer falls on you."

It took a few minutes to get through to Compoz, but his sleep-thick voice consoled me. "I've contacted the night supervisor at Mountain Bell. We'll have a readout on that incoming phone number by morning. I've posted patrol cars at the apartment, front and back. Try to think positive, and get some sleep. Tomorrow we're gonna break this case."

I must have believed him, because I fell into a hard, dreamless sleep that fooled me with its safety. No one disturbed me until almost noon on Tuesday.

The Sergeant didn't care about my receiving him in my robe. His mind was on the printout in his hand. "We got the number, Nyla. A pay phone on Grant and Fourteenth. About ten steps from the Capitol parking lot. Vice tells me it's a regular hotline to the Shallows. We're gonna pick up that blond tonight."

"Perhaps you can round up A.J. Farrell too. I haven't seen him since I went to his apartment and found the smashed coffee table. I don't have a good feeling about that." I informed him of the names that matched up on Bob Ross's list.

"I'll head over to Farrell's now. And I'll let you know what we find out from the blond."

When he left, I called Bob Ross. He wanted to know all the new details on Pat's case. I wanted to know who had had access to the interview notes for his research project with A.J.

"To my notes, no one. I guarded that stuff like a hawk. Tried to impress the need for confidentiality upon A.J. But I suppose any of his frat buddies could have seen the notes. He probably didn't think they'd be interested."

I dialed information, got A.J.'s number, and called his apartment. No answer. I figured Compoz would check the TKE house when he found him not at home. I wondered where A.J. worked. I even called the *Law Review* office, but Mr. Farrell was nowhere to be found. I didn't like the feeling that his absence might not be voluntary.

While I dressed, intending to go to Presbyterian, Tony and Audrey Louise joined me. "I made you brunch," he said proudly.

"Scrambled Eggs a la Zealot," Audrey Louise teased. "Compoz get the trace?"

I nodded. "They're picking up the blond kid tonight. I hope he'll tell us something."

"Sorry you got that scary phone call," Tony said. I looked at his mother.

"The cruisers were still on guard this morning. So we told the boys about it."

"Will you get a bodyguard?" the boy asked.

I considered it a helluva good idea. "I doubt it. I'll just have to be careful."

He pondered me while I ate my eggs. I liked how he looked in his thoughtful pose — his was the face of a future reporter, another justice-chaser. I could see it in his eyes.

159

Audrey Louise reminded him that we had to get to the hospital, and he jumped up to collect the brunch tray. He lifted my plate. "Here's a letter for you. And I wondered . . ." His shyness descended. "Tomorrow there's a big new fish tank opening at the Natural History Museum and um, well, they've also got a kite show. Do you think we could . . . um, that is, would you go with me?"

"Will this be our first official date?"

He blushed instant scarlet and I regretted teasing him. "Of course I'll go."

He scooped up the tray. "It opens at nine, so let's get there early."

I loved the softness in him, caught Audrey Louise watching us. "You're a fan," she said.

"Why not — he's going to make a great wife someday."

She pushed at my arm and told me to meet her down at the car. I tore into the envelope, relishing the sight of Lucy's familiar handwriting: *Watched the dawn yesterday, waited to see the color that is you. Something off the palate — what color is lightning? I look for you on all my horizons.*"

Sandal was the first of us back at the hospital. A fine powder of plaster dust had sifted into her hair and eyebrows. "I worked all night, too buzzed up to sleep. Rose is out for a walk, but she won't be long. Dr. Powers is due."

They converged shortly, the doctor looking the worse for wear. Sandal took Rose's hand.

Dr. Powers said, "I wish I had better news, Mrs. Stevens. Nothing is working to stop Pat's seizures, or equalize her intercranial pressure. Surgery is not a safe option. Unfortunately, without it there is much greater danger of brain damage."

"Is there nothing you can do?"

Dr. Powers shook her head. "Stay vigilant. Count on Pat's own strength. And pray." She held Rose's eyes a moment. "I'll check back later."

Minutes ticked off into interminable hours. Rose walked the circle of the hallway, lost in her thoughts. Sandal smoked. Audrey Louise left us about five o'clock to make dinner for her family. My mind felt empty and sore. I slipped into the chair next to Sandal and asked about the Amazon.

"You don't usually get two chances in stone," she said from the wreath of smoke settled atop her poncho. I imagined her standing before the battered granite, redrawing a line in her mind, finding a form within a form. "I did this time. She will spring forth, scars and all. May be my best work."

"Is Gladdie guarding her for the day?"

"She was bushed so I let her sleep in. How'd you manage to sleep after that phone call?"

"Compoz sent troops."

Sandal went to call Gladdie about supper; Marty arrived, and we discussed the dismal prospects of dry meatloaf in the cafeteria. Both of us were surprised when Robin Gaither came down the hall.

"I thought I'd see if there's anything you need. Find out how I could help. Professor Stevens was a really good teacher . . ."

"Still is," Marty said. "She's hanging on, and so are we. We were just discussing dinner plans."

Sandal returned from her phone call. "Gladdie's been simmering black bean soup all day, and pondering those

161

bricks." She ran her eyes quickly over Robin. "She has some further thoughts. Why don't we all truck out to the studio for dinner?"

"I'll be glad to go out for anything you want," Robin volunteered. "If anyone's staying in town."

"Thanks," Marty said. "I don't have much appetite either way. But we appreciate your stopping by."

He hesitated a moment. "Has A.J. been here today? I can't track him down, we're supposed to have a frat meeting tonight."

"Maybe you can reach him through his job," I said.

"That's what's a little weird. I called there today and he didn't show. Hmm, well maybe he pulled an all-nighter studying and crashed somewhere else. He'll turn up eventually." He smiled, shook hands with Marty, and bid us good night.

Rose rejoined us, carrying a large white box. We encouraged her to come to dinner, but she refused. Told us to get a good night's sleep. "And have a few laughs for Pat and me." Her tired smile belied the steel of will within her.

Sandal departed; I told Marty I'd meet him downstairs. Rose queried me with her expression. "I just thought I'd go in for one more visit with you tonight," I said, and saw the gratitude in her eyes. She carried the white box like precious cargo into Pat's room.

The dull amber light over the bed cast a pall on Pat's slack face. She looked haggard from the seizures. Her hands were bound at the wrist by loose elastic straps to keep her from flailing out and hurting herself.

Rose leaned in toward her daughter, ran her finger underneath the wrist straps. "I saved this for you, honey." She opened the box and a fluffball of faded pink appeared. "Here she is, your favorite coat." She patted

162

the coat up near Pat's pillow by her shoulder, then kissed her cheek. She whispered, "Here's Nipple."

I had a message at the nurses station from Compoz. He answered on the first ring. "No luck finding A.J. But our chicken is a songbird. He's tricked with A.J. Sunday nights steady since early March."

"You hearing the same bells I am, Sergeant?"

"Yeah, the Ides of March bit — someone feels betrayed. The kid says they went out in the mountains sometimes, but he swears they weren't on Lookout Mountain this Sunday, and he didn't make any phone call last night. Says he never heard of the Foresters or any pink flyers. I might see how he feels about consenting to a polygraph before I spring him tonight."

In the waning sunlight on our drive up Lookout Mountain, I watched the twilight shadows glint silver, then swirl around blooms up in the thin air. Marty and I were both in a zone.

"Last night knock it out of you?" he asked.

I tried to smile. "I guess so."

"Sorry I slept through the call. Maybe it's outdated, but I wish I could have . . . well, I still want to protect my friends."

I touched his arm. "Many things old fashioned have merit."

Stone lions reclined on each side of the steps to the house. One with sad eyes but a proud ruff rested his chin on his paws. His lioness was turned toward him with a look between a snarl and a smile. Ancient graffiti coiled across their shoulders.

163

"You think they'd tell us we enter at our own risk?" Marty teased.

Gladdie answered the door, looking rested and lively. "Soup's on," she said with a laugh. We feasted on rich black-bean broth and cornbread. When we finished, she escorted us into the den and lit candles. Then she sat on thick pillows on the floor, arranged her red muu-muu around her legs, and held a yellow tablet in her lap.

"On rare occasions, I've received spirit messages through automatic writing. I don't usually know who sends the messages, but I do know who they're directed to. All day I've had a strong sense of someone wanting to come through in this manner, with a message meant for both of you."

Marty tried not to squirm. I waited, eager to know the message. Sandal lit a small twist of sweet grass, and the odor reminded me of campfires on the beach. Gladdie took deep breaths and shook out her fingers, then picked up the pen and closed her eyes. In a moment, she began to write.

Life is sets of doubles. Friends, enemies. Love, hate. Awake, asleep. Poets and warriors. Mirrors of the same. The test of the body is finished. A stone may have the last laugh. Chariots beware.

She set the pen down, took more deep breaths. Waited a moment, then said, "That's it." Sandal rubbed Gladdie's shoulders, and Gladdie shook her hands again as if flinging off water.

An odd sensation began inside me, stimulation of my pores one by one. I sensed each organ in my body, saw myself as no mirror could ever show — the pale blue, peaceful backs of my eyeballs, the slick mauve walls of my heart, the interior of one hand like a glove of velvet flesh.

"I feel weird," Marty said. "Like someone stuck my finger in a socket."

"I feel it too," Sandal concurred.

"That's good. Nyla?" I nodded. "We've made a complete connection. Like an electric circuit," Gladdie told us.

"Do you have a drink in the house?" Marty asked, and Sandal laughed.

"I think Professor Punker just had his cage rattled," I teased. "You must be used to this, Sandal, living with a psychic warrior."

Gladdie blushed.

Sandal brought us wine and glasses. "Berdache, the Indians call it. Mediator between spirit and flesh."

Gladdie took the wine offered. "The Indians also say berdache takes both sexes to bed."

"How progressive of them," Marty commented.

"Mae West was a spiritualist." Gladdie studied the tablet page.

"Do we need her to translate this message?" Sandal asked.

Marty and I also examined the words on the page. "Something familiar here," I said. "But I can't place it exactly."

"Damned paradoxical," Marty concluded. "What's this about the stone? And this last phrase sounds like a warning. Except I thought of Lois Stan because of the word chariot. For her wheelchair."

"That's it," I said. "What I feel, the familiar. As if she were looking on just as she did in college, amongst us poets and warriors. Awake, asleep — surely that means Pat."

"As does 'the test of the body is finished,' " Gladdie added. "I hope that's forecast of an end to Pat's seizures."

"Love, hate — that's our fight against the Foresters," Sandal said.

Marty nodded. "Yes, and we've had to search among our friends as if one of them was an enemy."

"I don't get the reference about the stone either," I said.

"I'll give it more energy when I'm rested," Gladdie offered. "Perhaps I'll get clarification."

We were all tired but elated, and we parted company still feeling that slight buzz of the spirit electric. On the porch, Gladdie stroked her lions, patted their sculpted hair. "Flamelocks mon leo. Thetis could turn herself into a lion." She rubbed one stone cat's nose. "Tonight I feel like a psychic warrior. Tonight I have a lion inside me."

"Home, Chariot," Marty joked as we pulled out of the studio driveway. Moonlight played off the aspen, the stars pierced the thick night and widened out the tunnel of the highway. I felt the pull of the spiraling road, a grounding back to Denver in the lights below us. I thought about Lois Stan and her chariot of fire. "*Steel wheels having flown,*" she'd once started a poem. "*I become a balloon over the sea, a mote in the eye of the moon.*"

We'd driven about two miles when a car pulled off a side road and careened in front of us. Marty hit the brakes. Our car pulled left, toward the pit of blackness down the cliff wall. He jerked the wheel to the right. We slid close to the rock face, then back in the center of the

166

road. The car ahead disappeared into a curve. Marty cursed, and sped up again.

As we pulled into the curve, the other car sat dead center in front of us. We nearly broadsided it. Marty swerved up on two wheels against rock, scraping a shower of sparks. The Toyota banged down hard, the underbody flexing with a sharp crack. When I looked back, someone ran out of the brush and jumped into the other car. "Look out, he's going to come at us from behind!"

We heard the engine rev up. Before we could gain any ground, the other car bashed the Toyota trunk, and we shot forward. Marty strained to steer. With another jolt from behind, we lunged toward the edge of the highway.

"Hold on, Nyla!" Marty jammed the brakes hard and spun the car onto a narrow dirt ledge between the road and the precipice.

The other car rocketed past, sucked into the darkness. We could see the ribbon of highway below — two twists in the road, and another curve.

"You see the driver, Marty?"

"No, did you?" He breathed hard.

I shook my head. "Is he gone?"

"I think so." The night was suddenly eerie and silent. Nothing moved on the road below. Then, in the moonlight, we could make out a car creeping back up the curve with its lights off. "Marty, get us the hell out of here!"

But he didn't move, just sat behind the wheel, watching tensely as the car drove slowly toward us.

A third car rumbled past, honking loudly in the curve. The sound echoed up the throat of the mountains. Then it was still again, as if ours were the only car out in that darkness.

"He's stopped, I think he's stopped." Marty strained to see. On the road below, the monster machine flashed its lights. We could see dust shimmer in their yellow glare. Like a cat that stalks a moth, the car made a slow U-turn. Then jammed forward into the curve with a squeal of tires. We could hear him speed-shifting and the grind of gears.

Marty sighed and slumped against the seat. I couldn't catch my breath. I'd lost it on the overlook when we careened to a stop at the edge of the universe, two wheels just shy of blind space crashing downward a hundred feet into rock and pine.

"I got a look at the car," Marty gasped. "It was an old Bel Air."

16
DANGEROUS MAGIC

I left a report with Dispatch for Compoz. I sighed with relief at the cruiser parked in front of the Landrys, and prayed the phone didn't ring with that voice in my ear, that messenger of hate. Finally I did sleep, without dreams.

Marty had already gone to class when the alarm went off. I remembered my date with Tony. And wondered why the Sergeant hadn't called. When I went over to the main house, Audrey Louise slid buttered toast toward me.

"Good news. I talked with Rose this morning. Pat's seizures have stopped. Her pressure readings are looking better."

"Bless you, Lois Stan," I said, then described our mini-seance and the automatic writing. "How can a stone laugh?" Audrey Louise queried as Tony and I left for the aquarium.

Our first stop was the kite exhibit. Tony reported that the hit of the show was Black Beauty, a kite shaped like a Phoenix butterfly with a hundred-foot wingspan. I walked with my hand on his shoulder, enjoying our closeness.

"You know what else?" he told me. "A woman designed it. I read that in the *Denver Post*. I read all your articles too."

As we entered the atrium, I wished I had Tony's few cares. No fears about being driven over a cliff or sledgehammered in an alley. No need to judge one form of love over another. His questions for the world were simple and safe. Mine were not. Where was A.J. Farrell? Who was the driver of the Bel Air? What if Marty hadn't kept the car on the road?

Fifty or more customized kites hung on either side of the atrium; Tony took his time with each one. Shyly he appreciated a unicorn design; both of us enjoyed a rectangular box kite that looked like a car, called the Caddy-Lak. One classic car reminded me of another, and I realized the spectrophotometry on the Imperial paint sample would be pointless.

When we reached the central portion of the atrium, he grabbed my hand. "Look, there it is. Isn't it beautiful?" Thirty feet above us, the huge butterfly kite shimmered, its breast like a piece of the sky. Fans blowing across it made the wings billow, showing the kite's magic. A fountain nearby rose every few minutes in great shoots of water that nearly touched Black Beauty's silk tail.

I thought of the kites on Pat's bedspread. Out where her spirit floated, perhaps she glimpsed the freedom kites know.

The new sea water aquarium consisted of a honeycomb of windowed cells built around a 90,000-gallon central tank. We plugged in earphones to listen to a taped lecture. Sluggish sharks bumped along the bottom of the tank near our feet. Hawksbill turtles flapped by at eye level like giant, lumbering underwater birds. Purple-tipped anemones waved their seductive fillia, and balloon fish ran up and down one side of the tank like bird dogs pacing in their pen. The panther groupers studied us closely. Razor-faced morays zoomed through the grasses without escort.

We ventured into other exhibit cells, drawn by the odd allure of the murky lighting. We didn't talk much, just peered into the tanks at damselfish, personifier angels, and Picasso tigerfish with long eyelashes. Blue tangs and yellow puffers swam next to the pennant butterfly, which Tony dubbed "peanut butter fish."

In the last cell of the aquarium, we stared at a slender bamboo shark with slitted, steel-blue eyes. It spit gravel at us from underneath a chunk of antler coral. Tony kept his distance. The tank facing the shark held piranha.

How small they are for such lethal creatures, hiding their treacherous teeth in blunt jaws. Their silver scales flashed like tiny mirrors. Tony stared at them a long time, then shook his head. "But they're so pretty," he said. "Like a lady's evening bag."

We stopped for root beer floats on the way home. Tony bubbled about his summer reading program. He'd found a really old book of knock-knock jokes, and lamented that the jokes had gone out of style. "At school they tell spaceship jokes. I don't think they're funny."

"You mean because Challenger blew up?"

He nodded, looking down into his root beer glass. "I watched it on TV." The sudden tears in his eyes brought forth my own. "You know that term, godspeed? Mom says it all the time. Well, I think that must be how fast those astronauts went to heaven."

Back in Aurora, Audrey Louise was up to her elbows in cookie dough. Sam and Mark watched, waiting for the rewards of the oven. "How was Black Beauty?" she asked Tony.

"Terrific. How come you guys aren't helping?" He tasted the dough. "Oatmeal, neato Mom. My favorite."

"Mine too," I said.

"Ours too," the other boys chimed in.

"St. Joan of Oatmeal," Audrey Louise joked.

"Come on, you should help. It's really fun." Tony tied a dish towel around his shorts.

"It's sissy to cook," Mark declared.

"We're getting wives," Sam said.

Audrey Louise pointed to a note under a pineapple-shaped magnet on the fridge and said to me, "Phone message for you."

"Compoz?"

"Nope. The guy at Category Six. Neal, is it?"

Neal had called at Tell Parker's request. "They've tracked down Crazy Mary. You're to meet them at Cheesman. By the pillars, two o'clock."

I joined the cook's brigade, and we plopped out seven pans of cookies. We had so much fun that eventually

Mark and Sam relented, and helped in the baking. But they refused to wear anything resembling an apron. Afterward I took a swim with Audrey Louise; Tony put on his red-striped sunglasses and stretched out on the chaise lounge. At 1:30 I headed for the park.

By 2:15, Tell hadn't appeared. I waited another half hour, then trudged along the runner's path past every picnic table, porta-potty and clump of bushes. When I reached the Gauntlet, I almost went back to the car. After all the complaints to the Parks Patrol, I figured it was the last place Mary would be. Still, I forced myself to walk the distance of the cul de sac.

And there was Mary, barefoot and chomping a sandwich, her legs spread wide, her toes in the grass. When she saw me, she dropped the bread and scurried behind a tree.

"Mary, don't go. Please talk to me. I need your help."

She peered at me, rattling the handles on her shopping bags.

"Have you seen Tell today, or her sister? I was supposed to meet them here."

She giggled. "I seen 'em. Then I lost 'em."

"Hide and seek," I said under my breath. She took a step toward me. I realized I was standing next to the remains of her lunch. I sat down with my back to her. She took her spot again and finished the sandwich.

"Sorry about the cops chasing you. They just wanted to know if you saw anything related to the hit-and-run."

She chewed enthusiastically, but said nothing. Missed nothing with her eyes.

"My friend Pat is the womon who got hurt. I want to help her. I want to find out who ran her down."

Mary brushed at crumbs in her lap. "She gonna die?"

I waited to meet her eyes. "I don't know."

173

She looked away quickly, and surveyed the cul de sac. "This place is bad luck now." She plucked at the grass, worked her bare feet back and forth. "Good ole incinerator over there. No spiders." She pointed to a small brick quonset near the Rauch house. "Dry sleeping. But not anymore."

From the position of the incinerator, I could tell that if she'd been in it last Sunday night, she'd have had a clear view of the cul de sac. While no one would have seen her. But getting her to verify this would take some kind of magic. "How'd you get your brain for numbers, Mary? Neal thinks you're a regular wizard."

She reached into her triple bodice and pulled out half of a Baby Ruth. "With a number, you get things. Money out of a bank machine, phone calls, free bus rides. You can keep track — how many soldiers killed in a war. Like Vietnam — only that wasn't a real number, was it? Numbers of the national debt — that's the biggest number of all. Everything adds up to zero, but without numbers, that's all you got anyway."

She crumpled up the wrapper and tucked it back in her top. I wished Tell would appear and give me some creative way to get the bag womon to give up the goods.

"There was a number here that day." She looked off into the trees, as if I were no longer there.

"What day? You mean the day Pat got hurt?"

"I watched her plenty. She always wore a silver jacket. I could keep track a her by lookin' for that silver."

"Did you see her in the cul de sac? Did you see the green car?" I tried not to unnerve Mary with my eagerness. But it was hard to make myself sit still and pluck at the grass like she was doing.

"I seen the car. Shark fins on it. Blondy at the wheel. Then Silver showed up."

174

My heart did a drum roll. A bona fide eyewitness. "What else, Mary? Did she see him? Did he start up the car —"

She glared at me and shifted restlessly, glanced at her bags stashed in the trees. I shut up.

"He called out to her, but she didn't want nothin' to do with him. He follered her a ways, left the car door open. I made my move, to check out the back seat. Mighta been some burgers in there, or a sweater. He could spare it." Her eyes glittered. "That's when I seen the number. On the car door. I never knew they put one there."

I didn't understand about the number. "What about Silver and Blondy? Did you hear what they said?"

"She just gave him her back. That riled him up. Blondy ran back toward the car, so I had to hightail it." Mary stood up, started walking toward the trees.

"Wait, Mary, what happened after that?" I followed her, felt myself shaking with anticipation and hope.

"I sure liked that silver jacket," she said, rummaging in a Saks bag.

"Mary, *please.* Did you see what happened to Silver?"

She jerked her head up, her mouth a grim line beneath loden eyes. "He rolled that damn big car right over her like a bug."

I had a hell of a time coaxing Mary into my car. "I don't want nothin' to do with cops," she insisted.

I drove to the CNB office. The receptionist nearly popped her eyeballs at Mary's zebra-striped housedress and green plastic shoes. Mary, oblivious, pushed up her aviator sunglasses with her purple gloves, and kept a wary eye on her bags. "How long's this gonna take?"

I gave Bead the quick skinny; she agreed to stall our catch so I could alert Compoz. "She keeps talking about a number. Says she saw a number on the car door that day."

Bead's eyes flashed. "Hell, she *is* a wizard. That's a VIN number. Vehicle Identification Number. Positive I.D. With that, you can find your Bel Air."

Dispatch informed me that the Sergeant was out on a call, so I left a message. Bead coaxed the VIN number out of Mary: 1933-67-N-101856-1.

"Nineteen-thirty three, year I was born," Mary announced. "Then there's sixty seven — age my bastard uncle died. He lived too long, I can tell you. N is for no bargain bread at Safeway on Sunday. Ten-eighteen-fifty six, that's Martina's birthday." She made a motion, perfect tennis forehand. "Then Number One, that's me. A-OK, I'm the one I can depend on." She grinned proudly.

Bead grinned even bigger. "I'm getting a camera. This story will be a show stopper."

Since I couldn't reach Compoz, I tried Roy Dugan. Told him about the VIN number.

"I can run that down with DMV in a few minutes."

I was dancing out of my shoes with a buzz of body electricity — from Lois Stan and her flying wheels, Black Beauty ruling the skies, my own lion roaring inside me. And the wizardry of Crazy Mary.

Dugan rang right back. "We got a bingo on this. Right off that list we ran out before. Levere Eller's Bel Air."

While Mary posed for Bead's photos, I corralled Detective Franz. Still in his rumpled suit, he came to the office and took her statement. Listened with patience and consideration. Shook her hand and thanked her for the help.

"Mighty polite for a cop," she declared after he left. I drove her back to the park, and watched her stride into the trees — the true queen of Cheesman beach.

The unmarked Caprice crowded Joel's Saab in the driveway. Compoz sat poolside with his sleeves rolled up. The boys were gaga over his holstered .38. Joel speared franks on the grill.

"This is great, Sergeant. I get you positive proof, all you do is hang out by the pool in the burbs."

"What positive proof?"

"VIN number on the Bel Air." I described my unusual source.

"Can't wait for her to testify." He laughed, and flipped me a beer from a nearby cooler. "Guess this means Eller didn't turn his car over to the uncle in Grand Junction. I'll follow that up tomorrow."

"Where you been all day?" I asked.

He swigged his brew. "Denver's had several other crimes lately. My department frowns on my ignoring that. But as a matter of fact, I tried to find Farrell. No luck so far, but I had an interesting call from his buddy Gaither."

"Seems A.J. is out of touch with everyone," I said. "Robin came by the hospital last night looking for him."

"His sudden absence is starting to bother me." He shifted his holster. "Gaither asked us to make an official check at A.J.'s apartment since he hasn't shown up anywhere in two days. Said he was worried something might have happened."

"Had anyone cleaned up the coffee table?"

"No, it was still in a heap in the living room. Nothing else seemed disturbed; no sign of Farrell heading for the border. But we did find something I'll want him to explain when he shows up."

"Like what?"

"Three cans of red spray paint."

Marty invited Audrey Louise to play bridge at Patience and Sarah's, and so the two of them sashayed out for the evening. I sat in the apartment awhile, staring at the torn Polaroid. Then I plunked myself down in the hammock on the deck and let night whisper in around me. My thoughts moved with the sway of the hammock.

Life was full of doubles, all right. Poets and warriors in the same spirit, mirrors of each other. Like Pat and I trading places after all these years. An old friend found, then lost again into sleeping death. A brother and a lover — alive one day, then gone forever. A bag lady who was a numbers wizard. Flesh-eating fish pretty as a beaded evening bag.

We had doubles of blonds too — A.J. and the prostitute. More than doubles, since Robin was also blond. Palominos, golden horses . . . all those golden boys. Friends, enemies . . . pal-o-mine. I stared at the photograph. Not at the boy's face, but at the background — the ruins of a cabin shored up with bricks and boards. "We have a special place up at Sandhorn Lake . . ."

Just as the sky archer slipped into her necklace of stars, all the pieces of the puzzle fit. I knew who broke the coffee table and tore the picture. Who led the Foresters, and where the Bel Air was hidden.

17
SET UP

Three a.m., and I was still awake, trying to decide on a plan. Should I go up to Sandhorn Lake with an armed guard, or quietly confirm for myself that Eller's car was stashed at the TKE shack? A taped confession would be best, but I surely wasn't risking that without backup.

Audrey Louise had come home about ten without Marty. Maybe he'd met someone at the coffee house. His first date in years — I wished him well. When I heard a

179

quiet knock at the door, I wondered why he was being so polite.

Under the light, A.J. Farrell looked like a stand-up punching bag. Both eyes were blackened, and he hugged his ribs. "Had to talk to you . . ." He sagged against the doorframe.

"Get in here." I guided him to the couch. "No wonder you've been lying low." I grabbed a dish towel and emptied an ice tray into it. I handed it to him, wasn't sure which part of him needed it most. He tried to hold it to one cheek, but his arm trembled. "I'm not in on it," he said. "You gotta believe me. I'd never do anything to hurt Pat or Dr. Evans." He leaned his head back against the couch and closed his eyes.

He didn't look like anyone who could sledgehammer an Amazon. I asked, "Why did you lie to the cops about where you were when Pat was injured?"

"I was with Robin. I didn't want to get him mixed up in anything —"

"Cut the crap, A.J." I flipped the pasted together Polaroid toward him.

He clutched his ribs and sat up. Stared at the photo. "You know everything?"

"I know why you lied about your hours at the Capitol, about having a tutor. I know where you spend your Sunday nights. But not about Eller. Why'd you tell me you didn't know him?"

He shifted position, wincing. "I didn't really, except as a troublemaker. He got buddy buddy with Robin, and that was bad medicine. Robin changed — I knew he was having other guys do his classwork. But him with Eller, they fed something in each other. Robin acted like he had a bad taste in his mouth for the whole world."

180

"You and Robin have been using each other for a long time, haven't you?"

He sighed, as if the last of his energy had drained out. His eyes teared, but he said nothing.

"You were his ticket into a law firm, you had the brains. He had the brawn, the masculinity. No one would suspect either of you. Him of not making the grade. You of being homosexual."

"He's my best friend." He sobbed with the declaration.

"Not any more. He led the cops to your apartment and the cans of red spray paint he'd planted there."

His eyes blazed a moment, then blanked out. He put his head in his hands.

"You going to take the rap for him, or help me? You must know he's the ringleader."

"But why, why would he do it?" he choked.

"Whether you believe it or not, you've got a chance, A.J. Gay or straight, you can make something of your life. Robin's life ended when his sports career ended. Til he saw a second chance in you, riding your coattails into a lucrative law partnership. But not if your homosexuality was discovered. He saw the dollar signs falling away when you fell away, into the Shallows. When did he find out?"

"I think he suspected almost from the time I started . . . when I met Dean."

"The blond kid?"

He nodded. "Robin started hanging out with Eller again. Revving up the old hostility. He never liked me running with Pat either, always made remarks. Said it would rub off on me."

"He stomp in your coffee table?"

"Yeah, when he found the picture in my car. He hated that I took Dean up to the TKE cabin."

181

"So he chewed you up and spit you out. Once you were out of the game plan, you made a good pawn. After he sledgehammered the sculpture, he left the cap with the blond hair in it, then made the phone threat from the Shallows to point further suspicion at you. The spray paint nearly sealed the deal. Some stroke of luck for him, finding out where Marty and I would be so he could try to run us off the road."

A.J. went white, looked like he might faint. "Robin has to win at everything. No matter what."

Even if it kills someone, I thought. "You have a place to stay? Obviously you're not safe at your apartment or the frat house."

"I've been staying with Dean."

"Tomorrow you show me how to get to that cabin."

"All right." When he tried to stand, he wobbled against the couch. "Then what? Am I in trouble with the police?"

You should have come forward. If you had, Pat would be safe. I kept the thought to myself. Compoz would tell him soon enough. "We'll let them sort that all out, deal with Robin directly."

I was ready to go at daybreak, but mustered patience. A.J. wasn't in great shape — he'd need all the sleep he could get. I'd wait as long as I could, then call him at the number he'd left. When I phoned Compoz, Detective Franz answered. "Sorry, Nyla, Sal's not in. We got a Mexican standoff going. I expect he'll be out on that all day."

"Mexican standoff?"

"Barrio war off north Tejon. Hostage situation. Two officers down."

"I'm sorry."

"Yeah, it stinks."

A.J. surprised me by calling before nine a.m. "Robin's gone hiking for the weekend. Could you meet me at the frat house? I want to pick up some of my stuff. Then we'll go out to the cabin."

Downstairs, the station wagon was in the driveway, but no one was home in the big house. I borrowed the keys and left Audrey Louise a note. Marty could not be reached at his office. I wanted someone to know what we were up to, hoped I could leave directions to the cabin before we went there alone. I'd try calling again from the campus.

No red convertible in front of the TKE house; I pulled around to the empty driveway behind the carriage house. While I waited, I checked the garage. It was still overrun by the hulky Imperial. A.J.'s comment echoed in my mind. *Robin has to win at everything — no matter what.* I thought about Robin telling me, "We fix up the cabin just enough not to cave in on us." I realized I was standing in a brick carriage house. But when I looked for loose bricks, I found none inside. The building seemed to have been patched up with care.

It occurred to me that A.J. might be having second thoughts about helping me make a case against his best friend. I watched for the convertible outside from the far corner of the garage. In fifteen minutes, he still hadn't arrived.

As I turned to go toward the frat house, I noticed a small concrete mixer and several shovels leaning against the wall, along with a basketball backboard. The beginnings of a trench had been cut into the grass, disturbing a narrow, dirt-covered brick sidewalk. On the other side of the mixer I discovered a small pile of bricks. I rolled each one over carefully. Found three with the familiar frog — Don't Spit On the Sidewalk.

It seemed all the TKEs came from the same mold. The young man who gave me directions to the cabin was a sandy-blond who grinned a lot. "Watch that road in," he warned. "You can get high centered."

I stopped at a pay phone — still couldn't reach anyone, even at Dean's apartment. In exasperation, I dialed Category Six and gave Neal the brief details on my mission into the woods. "If I don't call in two hours, send the cavalry," I joked.

About forty miles outside Denver, I took the Windy Hill exit. Drove off the blacktop onto a gravel road that came out of a curve above Sandhorn Lake, shimmering cool and inviting in the sunlight. *Why not go wading instead? Wait for reinforcements.* I pulled over and checked my directions. I'd hit a dirt road on the other side of the lake, go on two miles, turn at a bright orange mailbox marked FOXES, and crank a hard left at three rows of lilac bushes. You had to beat the bushes to find this place. I hoped the station wagon wouldn't bust its oil pan on these pitted roads and leave me stranded.

At the lilac bushes, I drove on past the turn. Parked in a pine thicket out of sight. No madding crowd problems up here; the only things buzzing were bees on the flowers, dive-bombing for nectar.

Behind the bushes, I struggled through underbrush that had been piled up in a natural roadblock for non-TKEs. About sixty yards ahead, I saw the cabin filtered in shade, its door hanging askew. Up close, only one hinge anchored the door to the rotted frame. Behind it, darkness beckoned. A crow cawed; I jumped. Laughed at myself for the jitters. With a deep breath, I forged ahead into the cabin and nearly fell over a puncheon bench just inside. The place wasn't much to see — just one central room with crumbling walls and a dirt floor, a large trash barrel in the corner overflowing beer cans. And a makeshift fireplace constructed inside a circle of sooty bricks. I kicked them loose, and found several more ordinance bricks. *A stone may have the last laugh.* We didn't have Gaither's fingerprint, but the brick-bomb with soot traces would pin him.

Cracked timber shored up the ceiling beams, but the structure looked like it could topple in the first stiff wind. Or go up at the mercy of one loose match. I noticed a plank door in the back wall, figured it led outside. I was surprised to find it wedged shut. I pushed. The door gave a little. It wasn't locked, but had something heavy propped against it. I pushed harder, and the door gave. My shoulder banged up against the bumper of a rusty green car.

I had to drag aside a mountain of junk to get the driver's door open, but quickly verified Mary's VIN number. So this was Eller's '66 Bel Air. Behind it I also found a small tarp-covered mimeograph machine. In a burlap sack next to it I spotted a herald of pink Forester flyers. Dusty, but intact — more positive proof.

A car scraped through the low-hanging trees near the cabin. Wiping through grime at the window, I caught a glimpse of red. A.J. had come after all.

He entered the outer room, and I heard a small clatter of beer cans. "What happened?" I called to him. "Did we miss connections? I went to the frat house." I was halfway to the door when Robin Gaither stepped through it, and closed it slowly behind him.

"You beat out the cops, I'll give you that. I like a winner, at any game."

I made a run at him, and we wrestled against the Bel Air. Heat radiated out of him. I could smell beer. He pinned my arms behind me. "Nowhere to run anyway," he panted into my face.

"How fast did Pat Stevens run?"

"Not fast enough."

When he tried to shag a coil of rope, I jerked one arm free. Swung at him but he blocked me, sending a crackle of pain up my forearm. Before I could recover, he'd wrapped my wrists up tightly. Then he dragged me to the driver's side of the Bel Air and pushed me down into a rough crate.

"Where's your gang, Robin? They send you to do the dirty work all alone?"

He slammed the end of the rope in the car door and locked it. "Surprise, surprise. I'm a gang of one. Except for my little trip to Lookout Mountain, I fooled you all. Made you think there was a goddamned legion of us." He jerked the rope at my hands. "Sit tight, Nyla."

He rummaged in one of the junk piles, but I couldn't see what he was doing. Then I heard something tinny. Robin started to whistle. The dribble of liquid splattered onto the dirt floor. He moved back toward the wooden double doors, splashed them with the liquid. I smelled the pungency of gasoline.

With my face pressed against the car window, I could see Gaither pouring a large puddle under the Bel Air gas tank. He emptied the can into the car. "Fill 'er up."

From a shelf nearby, he picked up a soft-covered scrapbook and shook it at me. "Memories of the Foresters," he laughed. "I saved all the articles, even your stuff. The one from the *Post* when I redecorated that doctor's porch with bright red paint is my favorite. Too bad they didn't have the guts to run a photo. That's why I painted the letters so damned big."

He grinned, then laughed again. "Faggot Boy Lover, has a real ring to it."

"You're a helluva lot smarter than anyone figured, aren't you, Robin? Playing vandal, changing the tone and pacing of the notes. Mixing metaphors in the flyer — a little Bible-thumping, a little flag-waving. Committing the big crime and then the petty stuff to cover your tracks."

"Maniac queer haters on the loose! And everyone bought it. Thing is, I would have let the Foresters die a quiet death. We only had one semester before we could transfer to D.U. But Professor Stevens got in the way."

"She was A.J.'s friend. And she was on to you."

"Friend?" He smacked the side of the car. "You call someone who gives a guy the okay to screw teenyboppers up the ass a friend?"

"A.J. made that choice for himself."

"Yeah, that's what she said. I say be with queers, become queer. I told her to back off. She told me to jack off. I iced her, that simple." He flicked a cigarette lighter and ignited the scrapbook. "Besides, who cares? One less perv to worry about. You're their only crusader, and now you're going to fireworks heaven." He waved the small torch at me.

I started to jabber. "It got away from you, didn't it? Started out as a joke, a warning. Your new sport when you couldn't play football anymore. But this isn't one you can win, Robin. A.J. will tell the cops what he knows."

He laughed. "You think he's dicking a seventeen-year-old boy because he's proud of it? I'll expose him, ruin everything he's worked for. His old man will disown him." He tossed the torch inside a tire, and an old shirt flamed. "A.J.'s not gonna tell anyone anything."

Methodically, he lit a sack full of leaves, newspapers, and paint rags. I could see him taking his time to blow on the flame till it flared. "Ramshackle cabin, someone doesn't get their coals out. Happens all the time." He laughed low in his throat. Frantically I pulled on the rope as smoke sifted through the garage.

"I'm not here, Nyla. I'm camping in a grizzly haunt on Blue Creek. With three frat brothers who'll swear I never left them." He took the gas can and dragged the door closed. I heard the rattle of a padlock.

The leaves puffed a plume of smoke over the car. Burning newspapers ignited the gasoline; it whooshed high and hot. Crouched on the crate, I could see the flame snaking toward the back of the Bel Air. I jerked the rope till it bit through my flesh. Screamed for Lucy, but the acrid smoke made me cough and smothered my voice.

Oh god, I didn't want to burn. Down to melted hair and eyeballs, black muscles rubbery on bones under a ton of bricks. I'd be so much ash and Gaither would be laughing all the way to Blue Creek.

Timbers in the ceiling caught fire, spitting sparks down on me. The old paint on the garage doors flared in a hiss, and the tarp over the mimeo went up in a bright rasp. I jerked on the rope. Saw a roil of smoke from the puddle under the car. Time for my life to flash before my eyes.

A boot splintered through the side door just as the frame blazed like gunpowder. "Nyla, it's Tell Parker."

"Over here! I'm pinned in!"

She banged boards aside, fighting through the smoke and tangle of junk. The press of heat behind her made her hair look on fire. She slashed at the rope with a knife and dragged me onto my feet. Billows of choking smoke from the burning tires rolled over us. I could hear Scout yelling for her sister. Flames completely enveloped the garage. We could not go out the way she'd come in.

We stumbled toward the back of the garage. My eyes ached, I could feel myself turning to lava. We had only seconds before the car would blow. The double doors were a wall of flame. I could feel Tell's arms around me, and she yelled into my ear. There was nothing left to do. We ran into the fire.

18
TOUCAN

Burning wood snatched at my clothing. I felt the breath of a furnace in my hair, and a small burning at my eyebrows. Someone dragged me away from the cabin. My cheek skinned into wet grass, and I heard Tell fall next to me with a groan. Sirens clanged through the red hot air.

Gentle hands cradled my head. "Easy," Coral urged.

The firefighters yelled around us, "Foam that car down fast!"

"Is Tell okay?"

"She's pinked up like a lobster." She rocked me. I felt scraped and raw all over. I managed to sit up just as the side wall of the cabin collapsed like so much giant kindling. Over by A.J.'s convertible, P.D. and Gracie held Robin prisoner, his hands tied with a turquoise bandanna and another scarf at his throat.

A.J. and a sheriff's deputy punched through the wall of smoke. The officer eyed the guild. "Tough bunch," he said. "You ready for me to take charge?"

A.J. knelt beside me. "Nyla, I'm so sorry. I had second thoughts, but I didn't chicken out. I just got to the frat house too late."

Paramedics rolled Tell and me onto pop-up gurneys, and the lot of us rumbled back to Denver in an ambulance.

At Presbyterian, a resident M.D. rubbed my scorched eyebrows with vaseline. "I feel like I've been breathing in angel hair," I mumbled.

The doctor put me on oxygen. How wonderful to float in the quiet white of pure air. A cool hand upon my forehead brought me back to Earth, and Audrey Louise. "You scared me spitless." She kissed me.

A few minutes later, I knew I'd live. Other faces brightened around me: Marty, Rose and Sal Compoz. "You're a damned fool," Compoz said, trying to sound annoyed. "Lucky to be in one piece."

"What about Gaither?"

"I think we'll get a quick arraignment. A.J.'s already made a statement, and we saved the Bel Air so we can match up everything: paint, rust, the fender dent and the tire prints. Gaither conned a frat brother into that raid on the studio, and the kid is scared enough to confess to anything. Now all we have to do is find Crazy Mary and clean her up a little."

Rose had even better news. "Pat's out of ICU. Her brain readings are normal."

"Could she be coming out of the coma?"

"All signs are good."

I cried with relief. She patted my arm. Audrey Louise held one of my hands, while Marty squeezed the other. "Coming out," he said. "We do it all our lives."

By evening I had my land legs back. I wanted to see Pat for myself. The moment I stepped into her room, I felt something different. Knew she was coming back to us from the strata of kites. Marty strung Christmas lights around her door; Audrey Louise bought party hats and champagne. Rose asked us to drive her over to Pat's apartment so she could bring back the small painting of the golden surf.

Perhaps we willed her back, out of sleep and out of the doubles that had bound us all for these brief, violent weeks. For awaken she did, telling us she felt she'd been swimming in ether, through portals edged with the blue-black of cosmic night, and a sea of ochre tears — with Lois Stan ahead of her in a flying wheelchair. She broke the surface under a bower of spears held by wimmin warriors who flicked her with their courage.

We cried over her and touched her, to be sure she did not slip away again. When she wanted to sleep, we were afraid. Dr. Powers gave reassurance.

Pat was able to talk more on Friday, and told us about the confrontation in the Gauntlet. Gaither accused her of recruiting A.J., threatened to expose her at the college. She'd laughed at him. "They've known about me for years. And soon they'll know about you. Your harassment and the academic bribes. A.J. won't be your gravy train anymore."

Rose helped prop her up with pillows as Pat continued. "Here was this kid pressing all my buttons. But something cracked open. The old fearless me, before Lou." She shook her head, reached for her mother's hand. "The last thing I remember was the sound of my feet hitting the pavement, then something like a jet blast roaring up my back."

She loved the Christmas lights. We each told her our part in the escapade of rescue, and praised the missing heroes: Crazy Mary in her disco gloves, Sal Compoz and Roy Dugan, Neal and Dan, Gene Nile and Bob Ross. The Sisters of the Scarves, surely off somewhere protecting the fragile peace with their turquoise ferocity. Gladdie gave her Lois Stan's message in a frame designed with gilt lions. Sandal promised a special viewing of the Amazon. For a moment, we recaptured the vibrant aliveness of the Passionate Few.

"You're poets and warriors all, nothing more true," Pat declared.

"Except daughter lost and daughter found," Rose said, blooming with hope.

In my last sitting at the CNB office, I delivered to Bead the final story about the Foresters, written in a burn of focus that emptied me out. Justice had been served. Everyone survived. And everyone found a part of themselves changed.

I'd had my trial by fire without being consumed. I realized that my effort in and of itself had been my best to offer, and enough. Maybe modern warriors are wiser — they know all the battles count, large or small. They know we win by degrees, by love and truth and faith. Or so I told A.J. when he came to see Pat.

"No one says you have to march in the streets. Or bare your soul to strangers. But to your friends, you always owe the truth. If we deny it to each other, or hide from it, we can never be safe, or truly proud."

On my last night at the Landry's, Audrey Louise and I had margueritas by the pool. I told her about the destruction of the Burnton Wimmin's Center, how the fire had scorched my spirit with self doubt and created estrangement with Lucy. I told her about Judge Carruthers and the duty of the long spear. "I thought I'd dropped it somehow, or lost it."

Audrey Louise hugged me and petted my singed eyebrows. "My favorite zealot," she said, and kissed my nose.

Marty packed his belongings, and presented me with a copy of Ronnie's poems that he'd inscribed. Gave me a final bearhug, then headed back to the mountains to reclaim his home.

I read what he'd written inside the book. "Welcome back, Nyla Wade. Our new horizon jumper, our warrior of love."

On Saturday, I stopped by the hospital on my way to the airport to pick up Lucy. When I put the turquoise notebook back into Pat's hands, both of us gushed tears of joy.

"I think I will write again," she said. "But not about warriors or the womon-river. Will you be disappointed?"

195

"Nothing can change the time we had before. Now we make new discoveries. We know the fight is forever. But we never journey alone."

"I dreamed," she told me. "A lot about Stephen. I never saw him exactly, but I know he's at peace. In one dream, a lake of fire turned to ice, like a huge plate of quartz. I scooped up handfuls of the crystals; they made castles and planets and stars that fell through my fingers. A light wind over the water blew the ice into music, a magic chime." Tears splashed onto her pale green gown. "That was the essence of Stephen. Sending grace notes from the portals."

The fates had delivered Pat back to us and to herself. When I left her, I felt the wound of doubt inside me close up, healed by our sharing. I hoped one day soon she'd send me her first new poem folded inside a paper rose. She was the hotspur of my past. Now the womon of my future awaited.

At the airport, I wandered into a gift shop, found to my delight the ceiling festooned with satin birds. They twirled gently on their wires, flashing exotic tails and wings. One with a yellow breast and lime green beak caught my eye. My Satiness — I thought of touching Lucy, that satiny wet place of her surrender. My hotspur — her mouth at my breasts a small fire. Thought of Pat's dream, and knew another healing was at hand. No matter what burned up around us, Lucy and I would find the hot bright core of us again, magic as that lake of fire and ice that turned into music and new planets.

I bought the bird for her as a gift.

"Toucan," the clerk informed me.

Yes, I know.

A few of the publications of
THE NAIAD PRESS, INC.
P.O. Box 10543 ● Tallahassee, Florida 32302
Phone (904) 539-9322
Mail orders welcome. Please include 15% postage.

DOUBLE DAUGHTER by Vicki P. McConnell. 216 pp. A Nyla
Wade Mystery, third in the series.   ISBN 0-941483-26-6 $8.95

HEAVY GILT by Delores Klaich. 192 pp. Lesbian detective/
disappearing homophobes/upper class gay society.
                                           ISBN 0-941483-25-8   8.95

THE FINER GRAIN by Denise Ohio. 216 pp. Brilliant young
college lesbian novel.   ISBN 0-941483-11-8   8.95

THE AMAZON TRAIL by Lee Lynch. 216 pp. Life, travel & lore
of famous lesbian author.   ISBN 0-941483-27-4   8.95

HIGH CONTRAST by Jessie Lattimore. 264 pp. Women of the
Crystal Palace.   ISBN 0-941483-17-7   8.95

OCTOBER OBSESSION by Meredith More. Josie's rich, secret
Lesbian life.   ISBN 0-941483-18-5   8.95

LESBIAN CROSSROADS by Ruth Baetz. 276 pp. Contemporary
Lesbian lives.   ISBN 0-941483-21-5   9.95

BEFORE STONEWALL: THE MAKING OF A GAY AND
LESBIAN COMMUNITY by Andrea Weiss & Greta Schiller.
96 pp., 25 illus.   ISBN 0-941483-20-7   7.95

WE WALK THE BACK OF THE TIGER by Patricia A. Murphy.
192 pp. Romantic Lesbian novel/beginning women's movement.
                                           ISBN 0-941483-13-4   8.95

SUNDAY'S CHILD by Joyce Bright. 216 pp. Lesbian athletics, at
last the novel about sports.   ISBN 0-941483-12-6   8.95

OSTEN'S BAY by Zenobia N. Vole. 204 pp. Sizzling adventure
romance set on Bonaire.   ISBN 0-941483-15-0   8.95

LESSONS IN MURDER by Claire McNab. 216 pp. 1st in a stylish
mystery series.   ISBN 0-941483-14-2   8.95

YELLOWTHROAT by Penny Hayes. 240 pp. Margarita, bandit,
kidnaps Julia.   ISBN 0-941483-10-X   8.95

SAPPHISTRY: THE BOOK OF LESBIAN SEXUALITY by
Pat Califia. 3d edition, revised. 208 pp.   ISBN 0-941483-24-X   8.95

CHERISHED LOVE by Evelyn Kennedy. 192 pp. Erotic
Lesbian love story.   ISBN 0-941483-08-8   8.95

LAST SEPTEMBER by Helen R. Hull. 208 pp. Six stories & a
glorious novella.   ISBN 0-941483-09-6   8.95

THE SECRET IN THE BIRD by Camarin Grae. 312 pp. Striking, psychological suspense novel. ISBN 0-941483-05-3   8.95

TO THE LIGHTNING by Catherine Ennis. 208 pp. Romantic Lesbian 'Robinson Crusoe' adventure. ISBN 0-941483-06-1   8.95

THE OTHER SIDE OF VENUS by Shirley Verel. 224 pp. Luminous, romantic love story. ISBN 0-941483-07-X   8.95

DREAMS AND SWORDS by Katherine V. Forrest. 192 pp. Romantic, erotic, imaginative stories. ISBN 0-941483-03-7   8.95

MEMORY BOARD by Jane Rule. 336 pp. Memorable novel about an aging Lesbian couple. ISBN 0-941483-02-9   8.95

THE ALWAYS ANONYMOUS BEAST by Lauren Wright Douglas. 224 pp. A Caitlin Reese mystery. First in a series.
ISBN 0-941483-04-5   8.95

SEARCHING FOR SPRING by Patricia A. Murphy. 224 pp. Novel about the recovery of love. ISBN 0-941483-00-2   8.95

DUSTY'S QUEEN OF HEARTS DINER by Lee Lynch. 240 pp. Romantic blue-collar novel. ISBN 0-941483-01-0   8.95

PARENTS MATTER by Ann Muller. 240 pp. Parents' relationships with Lesbian daughters and gay sons.
ISBN 0-930044-91-6   9.95

THE PEARLS by Shelley Smith. 176 pp. Passion and fun in the Caribbean sun. ISBN 0-930044-93-2   7.95

MAGDALENA by Sarah Aldridge. 352 pp. Epic Lesbian novel set on three continents. ISBN 0-930044-99-1   8.95

THE BLACK AND WHITE OF IT by Ann Allen Shockley. 144 pp. Short stories. ISBN 0-930044-96-7   7.95

SAY JESUS AND COME TO ME by Ann Allen Shockley. 288 pp. Contemporary romance. ISBN 0-930044-98-3   8.95

LOVING HER by Ann Allen Shockley. 192 pp. Romantic love story. ISBN 0-930044-97-5   7.95

MURDER AT THE NIGHTWOOD BAR by Katherine V. Forrest. 240 pp. A Kate Delafield mystery. Second in a series.
ISBN 0-930044-92-4   8.95

ZOE'S BOOK by Gail Pass. 224 pp. Passionate, obsessive love story. ISBN 0-930044-95-9   7.95

WINGED DANCER by Camarin Grae. 228 pp. Erotic Lesbian adventure story. ISBN 0-930044-88-6   8.95

PAZ by Camarin Grae. 336 pp. Romantic Lesbian adventurer with the power to change the world. ISBN 0-930044-89-4   8.95

SOUL SNATCHER by Camarin Grae. 224 pp. A puzzle, an adventure, a mystery — Lesbian romance. ISBN 0-930044-90-8   8.95

THE NESTING PLACE by Sarah Aldridge. 224 pp. A
three-woman triangle—love conquers all!   ISBN 0-930044-26-6   7.95

THIS IS NOT FOR YOU by Jane Rule. 284 pp. A letter to a
beloved is also an intricate novel.   ISBN 0-930044-25-8   8.95

FAULTLINE by Sheila Ortiz Taylor. 140 pp. Warm, funny,
literate story of a startling family.   ISBN 0-930044-24-X   6.95

THE LESBIAN IN LITERATURE by Barbara Grier. 3d ed.
Foreword by Maida Tilchen. 240 pp. Comprehensive bibliography.
Literary ratings; rare photos.   ISBN 0-930044-23-1   7.95

ANNA'S COUNTRY by Elizabeth Lang. 208 pp. A woman
finds her Lesbian identity.   ISBN 0-930044-19-3   6.95

PRISM by Valerie Taylor. 158 pp. A love affair between two
women in their sixties.   ISBN 0-930044-18-5   6.95

BLACK LESBIANS: AN ANNOTATED BIBLIOGRAPHY
compiled by J. R. Roberts. Foreword by Barbara Smith. 112 pp.
Award-winning bibliography.   ISBN 0-930044-21-5   5.95

THE MARQUISE AND THE NOVICE by Victoria Ramstetter.
108 pp. A Lesbian Gothic novel.   ISBN 0-930044-16-9   4.95

OUTLANDER by Jane Rule. 207 pp. Short stories and essays
by one of our finest writers.   ISBN 0-930044-17-7   6.95

ALL TRUE LOVERS by Sarah Aldridge. 292 pp. Romantic
novel set in the 1930s and 1940s.   ISBN 0-930044-10-X   7.95

A WOMAN APPEARED TO ME by Renee Vivien. 65 pp. A
classic; translated by Jeannette H. Foster.   ISBN 0-930044-06-1   5.00

CYTHEREA'S BREATH by Sarah Aldridge. 240 pp. Romantic
novel about women's entrance into medicine.
                                         ISBN 0-930044-02-9   6.95

TOTTIE by Sarah Aldridge. 181 pp. Lesbian romance in the
turmoil of the sixties.   ISBN 0-930044-01-0   6.95

THE LATECOMER by Sarah Aldridge. 107 pp. A delicate love
story.   ISBN 0-930044-00-2   5.00

ODD GIRL OUT by Ann Bannon.   ISBN 0-930044-83-5   5.95

I AM A WOMAN by Ann Bannon.   ISBN 0-930044-84-3   5.95

WOMEN IN THE SHADOWS by Ann Bannon.
                                         ISBN 0-930044-85-1   5.95

JOURNEY TO A WOMAN by Ann Bannon.
                                         ISBN 0-930044-86-X   5.95

BEEBO BRINKER by Ann Bannon.   ISBN 0-930044-87-8   5.95
               Legendary novels written in the fifties and sixties,
                    set in the gay mecca of Greenwich Village.

VOLUTE BOOKS

JOURNEY TO FULFILLMENT	Early classics by Valerie	3.95
A WORLD WITHOUT MEN	Taylor: The Erika Frohmann	3.95
RETURN TO LESBOS	series.	3.95

These are just a few of the many Naiad Press titles — we are the oldest and largest lesbian/feminist publishing company in the world. Please request a complete catalog. We offer personal service; we encourage and welcome direct mail orders from individuals who have limited access to bookstores carrying our publications.